...of

"Like .... n satirist
with a .... *Who's Not*
is a thoroughly entertaining romp through the minefields of celebrity journalism, workplace intrigue, and the misguided human heart."

—Tom Perrotta, author of
Election and *The Wishbones*

BIG BABIES

"A hilarious novel ... frantically funny ... A brilliant satire, packed with coincidences and wry observations about contemporary American culture."

—*Publishers Weekly* (starred review)

DIMINISHED CAPACITY

"Entertaining ... a swift-flowing tale of low comedy and high jinks. Kiraly does an admirable job."

—*New York Times Book Review*

"Funny, utterly guileless, and friendly ... This is a fast, light book meant to be simply enjoyed. But unlike so many novels of a similar type, *Diminished Capacity* is extremely well written and has a real message about faith and courage ... A truly good-hearted novel."

—*Los Angeles Times*

"Kiraly captivates the reader with both his comic Midwestern sensibility and an eye for small-town absurdities. *Diminished Capacity* has it all: action, adventure, romance, and one amazingly preserved baseball card."

—Mark Steven Johnson,
screenwriter, *Grumpy Old Men*

"Fannie Flagg meets W. P. Kinsella ... whimsical, charming, and funny."

—*Kirkus Reviews*

Continued ...

CALIFORNIA RUSH

"Kiraly's scored a solid base hit."

—*New York Times Book Review*

"*California Rush* is not just a baseball book. It is a very entertaining story that should amuse even readers who are not fans of the sport."

—*Los Angeles Times*

"A rare treat . . . Sherwood Kiraly has swept a literary double-header. Not only has he written a delightful first novel, he has also written a delightful baseball novel. *California Rush* is a whimsical, light and loving look at baseball, and the author gets special applause."

—*St. Louis Post-Dispatch*

"A wonderfully told story, with well-drawn characters and a nice turn of phrase."

—*Library Journal*

Who's HOT Who's NOT

SHERWOOD KIRALY

B
BERKLEY BOOKS, NEW YORK

This is a work of fiction. The characters and events described in this book are imaginary, and any resemblance to actual persons, living or dead, is purely coincidental.

This book is an original publication of The Berkley Publishing Group.

WHO'S HOT/WHO'S NOT

A Berkley Book / published by arrangement with
the author

PRINTING HISTORY
Berkley trade paperback edition / December 1998

The Penguin Putnam Inc. World Wide Web site address is
http://www.penguinputnam.com

ISBN: 0-425-16530-2

BERKLEY®
Berkley Books are published by The Berkley Publishing Group,
a member of Penguin Putnam Inc.,
375 Hudson Street, New York, New York 10014.
BERKLEY and the "B" design
are trademarks belonging to Berkley Publishing Corporation.

PRINTED IN THE UNITED STATES OF AMERICA

10 9 8 7 6 5 4 3 2 1

Who's
Hot
Who's Not

Sherwood Kiraly

ONE

Officer Hundley interviewed us in the conference room. I was one of the first—not because of any great standing I had at the magazine, but because I'd known our employer the longest.

Officer Hundley was tall and heavy, with wispy blond hair and a mustache. He had a clipboard he took notes on, and he had a tape recorder in front of him on the conference table.

I was conscious of being extra natural as I sat across from him. I hadn't done anything to Harry Poe, but there I was, and there was the cop, and I don't know. If I'd been him I would have suspected me. I was pale and skinny and suspicious-looking. I'd always felt I could go bad at any time.

"You're Joseph Hoyle?" he asked, consulting his clipboard.

"Yes, right. Joe. Joseph."

"So," said Officer Hundley. "This is going to be according to Hoyle."

"Heh-heh," I said politely.

"And you are the"—he looked at the clipboard a moment dubiously—"head goon?"

"Well, that's a little informality there, on the masthead page, but yeah. I read the entire magazine just before it prints out. And check facts and corroborate things, and I locate people for the Where Did They Go? section. That's what we're called sometimes—goons. Actually I'm proud to be a goon," I finished, unnecessarily. He hadn't asked me if I was proud or not.

"You and Mr. Poe were in college together?"

"That's right."

"And he started the magazine."

"Founder, publisher and editor-in-chief," I confirmed. "There wouldn't be any *Who's Hot/Who's Not* without Harry Poe."

There are many entertainment magazines, with many who's hot/who's not sections in them, but there is only one *Who's Hot/Who's Not* magazine. It was Harry's idea to bring out a publication in which success and failure were split right at the staples every week. The two distinct sections—always an equal number of pages devoted to the hot and the not—distinguished us from the tabloids and other slicks. With our weekly, you could read the section that matched your disposition. If you wanted inspiration, you could focus on the success stories in part one. If, on the other hand, you thought it might cheer you up to read about the misfortunes of the prominent, you could turn to part two.

In the magazine's early days, Harry picked out all the hots and the nots himself, using a formula based on box office totals, Nielsen ratings, industry gossip and personal instinct. Later he delegated this responsibility to me, and when I burned out he gave it to Neil Purkey. Harry reserved final say on it for himself, though, and exercised this right fairly often.

My main responsibility these days, as I told Officer Hundley, was the final read and the Where Did They Go people. I rarely went out looking for anyone—I usually found them by phone—but I did all the background, uncovered little anecdotes about them and interesting cross-references. Harry liked me because I was careful. I had a neurosis about accuracy.

The public liked our magazine from the start. It was so clean-cut: winners in front, losers in back. Hollywood people bought it to see which section they were in. Harry had each issue wrapped in plastic so you couldn't skim it at the store. Two years after the first issue came out, there was even a weekly cable TV version on, in the early evening.

"We wouldn't be here if it weren't for him," I told Officer Hundley. "I especially wouldn't because he hired me personally when I was . . . when I was . . ."

I stopped. I didn't want to get into a long thing.

"When you were what?"

"Well, I was kinda down after I left school." I shrugged. "Had a period there where I didn't do too well. Harry hired me. I've been with him ever since."

The officer put his clipboard down and leaned back in his chair.

"What would you say is the opinion of Mr. Poe, here at the office? What do people think of him?"

"They think he's the boss."

"Do they like him?"

" 'Like,' " I said thoughtfully. "That's a pretty strong word."

"How about you, what do you think of him?"

I hesitated. The truth was that my attitude toward Harry was ambivalent—not the kind you want to work through with a policeman investigating his disappearance.

"If you had to describe him in a phrase," the officer encouraged me. "What would it be?"

This was an unusual cop, I thought. His questions were similar to what Barbara Walters might have asked.

"Uh, happy warrior?" I suggested.

He glanced at his clipboard.

"We've been told Mr. Poe forced a homeless woman into his vehicle while on the way to work so he could use the carpool lane."

The Carole Spangler incident. I sighed. Officer Hundley flipped a page.

"Did you, on that occasion, confront Mr. Poe in the office waiting room and call him a dickhead?"

My first thought was that this was typical of the kind of corrections I had to make every day.

"It wasn't the waiting room, it was the *weight* room." I mimed a curl.

"But you did call him this name."

"Well, I told you, we were in school together."

"Did you also say that someone should 'yank *his* wise ass off the street' so he could see how it feels?"

I scrunched around in my seat. I'd stopped smoking and I wanted at least a toothpick, but I didn't want to appear nervous.

"And then, the next day, Wednesday," Officer Hundley went on, "Mr. Poe didn't show up for work."

"Hey," I said.

I thought it was shortsighted of the officer to be focusing on me this way. I wasn't even one of Harry's enemies. Harry had real enemies to spare. He had an A, B and C list.

It wasn't that he was mean. It was just that he was oblivious. Our whole business is kind of marbled with insensitivity. When you expose people's failures and flaws for a living, you can become impervious to their feelings. The nature of the business is such . . . well, I'm making excuses. Harry didn't become insensitive in the course of running the magazine. He came in that way. Harry just had this attitude. Kind of happy-go-lucky. To him it was a game. Life was all stories and contests; he loved all that. We were all stories to Harry, all part of the pageant. He didn't seem to realize that some people take life personally. Consequently, where most people have a few individual enemies, Harry had sets.

Celebrities and ex-celebrities who had appeared in the Who's Not section had threatened him several times. Eddie Friend, the actor, once sent his personal assistant over to our office to beat Harry up. Eddie was too upset to do it himself. One of our production people, Jimmy Nations, went toe-to-toe with the guy right in the reception area.

It didn't rattle Harry, though. The very next day at lunch at

Cicada, he walked up to Eddie Friend's table and challenged him to overcome our publicity. I was there, and I heard it. So did the other lunchers. Eddie was taken aback and had nothing prepared; he just sat and stared up at Harry, who stood over the table at his full six-one, wearing his favorite tan coat, his blue eyes glinting behind his glasses, and harangued him, like this:

"Damn straight and hell yes, it's *hard* to get back to Hot after you've been in Not. This is a tough town. The typical progression is Hot to Not to Out of the Book. But that's the challenge! The ones with fire in the belly can go from Hot to Not to Hot. Look at Travolta. Some have gone Hot-Not-Hot-Not-Hot! Look at Sinatra! It made them bigger than ever, and stronger. You shouldn't be offended to be in Not—you should take it as a springboard back to Hot. And lemme tell you something. When you finally get that showy supporting role and these bastards realize you're not through, we'll be the first book to showcase you."

Harry came back to our table, sat down and murmured, "And will we get a thank-you? I don't think so."

In addition to the performers he had routinely offended over the years, Harry had recently widened his scope by coming up with an innovation. He had decided that in addition to the usual actors, rock stars and athletes we profiled, we would now include mutual fund managers.

The idea had come to him while sampling the slick financial magazines. "These people get photographed like Marlene Dietrich," he said. "And you know what else? They got everybody's money." For this reason, Harry believed, the public would become ever more interested in the fund managers as individuals. Also, they had positive and negative stats—the profit and loss of their funds. "We can quantify the hotness and the notness," he told me. He was enchanted with the whole idea. So he had expanded the New York office and we kicked off the new department with a cover box of James Steiger—the manager of the troubled Patrick Henry Value Fund—inebriated or looking it with a woman-not-his-wife

6 Sherwood Kiraly

outside a Manhattan club, under the banner, "A Fool and Your Money?" Initial reader interest had been gratifying. We'd heard from several outraged and apprehensive fund executives. Steiger himself had called and asked to speak to the odious parasite in charge.

Harry had another potential set of enemies among the twenty-eight employees at the L.A. office. Actually he was a good boss in some ways—generous, even inspirational. But he was mercurial too. Capricious. He'd give us all odd, impromptu quizzes and tests instead of formal job evaluations. Like he'd call you in and ask you to name the sexiest letter in the alphabet—the letter most likely to catch the eye of the average newsstand browser. And if you didn't guess one of his favorites (B, F, G, S or V), he'd go sour on you. People hate it when employers judge them on the basis of some oddball test.

About once a week he'd get very hands-on; he'd walk through each department like a commandant and look over everyone's shoulder. This meant that the lower-level employees, who would ordinarily resent their immediate superiors, often went over their heads and resented Harry instead.

He had a breezy way of criticizing you in front of everybody that could chafe a little bit, especially when he got your name wrong. Esther Tighe worked for us for five years and Harry mis-identified her when he fired her; he called her Emily. He was justified in letting her go, but just the same he should have fired her by her right name.

There was a group that got together on Thursdays after work and fantasized about introducing some anxiety into Harry's life. It wasn't all they fantasized about, but that theme was in there. Neil Purkey, Jimmy Nations and Emily Hahn, Harry's secretary, were usually in attendance, and me sometimes, because I liked those people.

Yasmine, Harry's second wife, was divorcing him on grounds of self-absorption, just as Bianca had. They got mad at him too.

To win them over originally, he had focused all his enthusiasm upon them. Then, with that job accomplished, he'd gone and focused it on someone or something else.

He really had pulled a homeless woman into his jeep, a week before—on the first day of October—to win a bet with Ernie Scheffing, one of our salespeople.

Harry, Ernie and I all lived in Laguna Beach, one to two hours south of the L.A. office, and Harry had offered to bet that he could give each of us a fifteen-minute head start on the drive up to work and still beat us. I wouldn't bet with Harry, but Ernie did. He'd only known him for about a year.

Harry's edge was that he'd seen this woman standing on the on-ramp to the 405 freeway for the last three workday mornings, holding a sign saying she'd work for food. So on the Tuesday of the race he came roaring up to her—first let me say that he didn't cheat; Ernie called him on his car phone at the fifteen-minute mark to make sure he was still home—Harry came skidding up to this woman, tossed her in beside him in the jeep, roared onto the 405 and over to the carpool lane and he was past Ernie before they got up to Long Beach.

When I got to work that morning, I went to see Harry about something we'd written about Steven Seagal and found him on a Cardiac Rider in the weight room attached to his office. My first view of the woman was of a shapeless lump in a big brown coat, sitting on a mat against the far wall. She looked sullen and bleary—red-faced, raggedy and bedraggled. I couldn't guess her age, although I felt confident that she was in the eighteen to forty-nine group.

Ernie Scheffing paced back and forth in front of Harry, who was rowing on the machine in a gray sweatshirt with cut-off sleeves. In college Harry had been overweight, but now, as an executive, he kept trim. He said that sometimes you had to be in good shape just to pick up a pen and sign your name.

Harry had an open, enthusiastic face behind his glasses. His eyes would sometimes widen in surprise at things he said himself. On this morning he was clear-eyed and serene, the winner again. Ernie Scheffing, on the other hand, was steamed.

"We said no carpool lane," Ernie insisted, frowning at Harry's sneakered feet. Ernie was a short, well-dressed salesman with gray-ing, curly hair. He told me once that he made his decisions about people by looking at their shoes. His own shoes were sharp.

"No, we said no driving illegally," Harry amended.

"It was understood that we would be driving alone," Ernie said.

"Understood by you."

"You said you were alone when I called."

"I *was* alone when you called."

The woman on the mat looked around at the weight room. She had brown hair over her forehead.

"Her name's Carole Spangler," Harry told us. "I told her she's free to use any of the apparatus."

"You cheated," said Ernie Scheffing.

Harry hauled on the machine's handlebars.

"You think?" he said mildly.

"Well, you took advantage of an assumption. I don't think I should have to pay," said Ernie, smiling uneasily.

Harry looked at me. He liked to refer to me on minor technical points—he said I was the only one in the building who knew how to spell "its"—and occasionally on questions of ethics. "Did I cheat?" he asked.

I stared at the woman on the mat.

"Did she want to come up here?" I asked.

Ernie Scheffing brightened.

"Kidnapping!" he declared. "That's driving illegally!"

"No it isn't," said Harry, bobbing up and down on the rider seat and shaking his head. "And anyway, I paid her. I hired her, to sit next to me on the ride."

"Bastard," stated the woman. It was the first thing she'd said. Her voice was scratchy. She really pronounced her R's.

"I explained to her," Harry continued, "that I was in a hurry, and I offered to let her out up here on Wilshire, but she wouldn't get out."

"I don't LIVE up here," the woman rasped out.

"Well, you don't live *any*where," Harry replied reasonably.

Right here is where I made the remarks which Ernie Scheffing later relayed to the police. As I did so, the woman rose laboriously and wobbled over toward the rowing machine. When she arrived, she wound up a big open-handed right and clapped Harry on the side of the head, getting a surprised "OW!" out of him. The force of the swing caused her to teeter, but I caught her and tipped her back upright.

She peered up at me, and we both recoiled slightly. She smelled of wine and sweat. Her eyes were red, white and brown. I smiled politely.

"Joe Hoyle," I said.

"Keep it in your pants," she replied.

Harry continued rowing. He never stopped rowing until he got to twenty minutes. Only now he was doing it cowboy style, one-handed, holding his other hand over his ear.

The woman stuck her tongue out at him and made a raspberry sound. Then she turned and waggled her rear end at all three of us in a disdainful kind of way. Finally, she walked back over to the wall and slid back to the floor.

"She's got a grievance, y'know," I told him as we all stared at her. "You yanked her right off the road."

"Hey, I paid her twenty percent of what I'm gonna get from Ernie here," he said. "Think she could've made a hundred doing anything else? She slept two-thirds of the way."

"I don't care," I said. "Everybody's not here on earth just for your goddamn convenience."

Harry held up a hand to stop me.

"Almost there," he said. When he reached twenty minutes he got off the machine, walked over to the woman and squatted down to address her.

"Do you know where you are?"

She looked around the gym again.

"You're at my magazine," Harry said distinctly. "*Who's Hot/Who's Not.*"

"What?"

"*Who's Hot/Who's Not.*"

Her eyes narrowed.

"You tryna be funny?"

"No. It's a magazine."

She glared blearily for a moment longer, then let her head go back against the wall.

"The Carole Spangler story is not for sale," she told him. "I've got some dingdity."

Harry rubbed his face.

"I'm sorry if I offended you," he said. "But I did pay you."

She scratched the outside of her pants pocket, doubtfully.

"I just needed you to be in the vehicle," said Harry.

"You just wanted my body." She laughed and coughed a bit. Then she focused on Harry. She ran her fingers over her tongue and flicked them at his face. "You may go," she said.

Harry stared at her.

"I'm gonna have to ask you to back off," she added. "You're interfering with my reception."

Harry's secretary, Emily Hahn, came in, stood over Harry and announced, "I won't be spoken to the way James Steiger is talking on the phone right now. If you don't take over, I'm gonna tell him off."

"Okay," said Harry. To Carole he said, "I have to go to work."

"You're dismissed," she replied.

Harry cocked his head to one side and looked at her, kind of puzzled.

"I haven't always been as you see me," she said.

He gazed at her for another moment. Even I got a little twinge, looking at her, and a fleeting thought: She's way too young to be Anastasia.

"Lemme talk to this guy," said Harry, "and then get back to you."

As he walked past me, he muttered, "See if she wants some iced tea."

He seemed suddenly impressed with her. I'd seen Harry act on impulse before. I wouldn't have been surprised if he'd come back and hired her. But as far as I knew, all he did that day was drive her back down south. She wasn't at her spot on the on-ramp the next morning when I drove by. By Monday I was talking to Officer Hundley.

· · ·

"You and Mr. Poe are neighbors, is that right?" the officer asked.

"Well, we both live in Laguna Beach, but Harry lives in a big place. Up the hill a mile or two from me. I rent. Harry bought this huge—used to be a monastery, then it was somebody's estate. It was gonna be torn down so he got a deal. He lives up there in the Top of the World neighborhood. We don't see each other much except down on the boardwalk, with our dogs. Harry loves his dog."

Officer Hundley seemed uninterested in this tidbit. He sighed, looking down at his clipboard.

"He's not as bad as he sounds," I went on. "He warned old Mrs. Armbrister when the fire was coming to Laguna in '93 and helped get her photographs out of her house."

Hundley sat back and looked at me.

"You're in charge of Where Did They Go," he said.

"That's right."

"Well? Where did he go?"

I shrugged.

"He could be somewhere in his house. I'm telling you, it's big."

"Okay. Last question: Does a particular, *outstanding* enemy come to mind?"

I grimaced and shook my head.

"You can't do a Top Ten because they keep changing positions."

The officer thanked me for my help and I left the conference room. Jimmy Nations got up from a chair in reception, wearing his production smock, and approached me. Jimmy was a nice, big, hotheaded kid, with peach fuzz and an open face. He smiled nervously.

"I'm next," he said.

"Don't worry," I told him. "He thinks I did it."

On my way down the hall, I saw Ernie Scheffing. He ducked into the men's room—the mark of the squealer. Back in my office, Neil Purkey was the first to come around, followed by the rest of the editorial staff and half of sales. There was a lot of speculation about Harry. Joanne Shaw appeared, collecting for flowers for Steve Kluszewski's wife, who was in the hospital with a bronchial problem. Joanne worked with Neil on the Who's Not section. She and I lived together for a while, but it threw us off. We got along better before we tried it.

"Have they found the body?" she asked merrily.

I felt myself getting annoyed for the first time all morning.

"You know," I said, "I'm kind of hamstrung here because I don't hate the guy as much as everybody else."

"Oh, it's not that," said Joanne. "It's just that nobody believes it. He's probably shacked up somewhere. Nobody thinks he's really dead."

Joanne went away with twenty dollars for Steve Kluszewski's wife. Neil gave me what he'd found on Bobby Vee, our Where Did They Go subject for the week. I put my scuffy shoes up on my

desk and looked at them. Harry didn't care what anybody wore
to work. I heard a commotion up toward the switchboard and
thought for a moment that he'd walked in, but it turned out to be
one of the salesmen, hollering about his messages.

Harry and I had outlived the buddy years. We had each been
married, me once, him twice. We each had our own crowd. Or I
should say, Harry had many crowds, and I had a few friends. If
we hadn't worked in the same office we'd have been at the bottom
of each other's Christmas card list.

But we were once best friends. Harry was the only person besides my parents who had ever actually saved my life. At home in
a box somewhere I had an old photo of the two of us. We were
twenty-two and twenty-one, standing on a snowy suburban Chicago lawn with our arms around each other's shoulders—pals.
Across the bottom, Harry had printed in marker: "Bonus Time."

The picture was taken by Harry's sister Kate, on the Poes'
front lawn in Western Springs. I was Harry's guest that year, on
our Christmas break from Peppard College in central Illinois. On
the previous evening, Harry'd been driving me around Chicago in
his dad's El Dorado, on a cold sleety evening, and we'd ended up
riding a restraining rail, looking down on the Eisenhower Expressway. I've told the story various times, but it was one of the two
or three moments in life that narrative really can't do justice to.
You'd have to have been in the passenger seat with me to get the
full flavor.

It was about 7:30. We'd been in the Loop all day, picking up
gifts, and Harry had been showing me the sights; I was the down-
state rube from Bloomington. We'd finished with a cheeseburger
at the Billy Goat tavern, a popular place under Michigan Avenue
where a lot of newspaper people in Chicago go, and now we were
leaving the city, on our way back to Western Springs. Harry'd only
had a couple beers and was functional, but the driving conditions
were bad—more icy than snowy.

We were halfway up this curving on-ramp to an overpass leading to the Eisenhower when the car hit a patch of ice, and we slid, smoothly, gracefully, sideways, to the right, while Harry frantically whipped the steering wheel this way and that. The car didn't respond to the wheel. We just kept sliding. Instead of following the road up and to the left, we were going over the side, off the overpass. The only thing in our way was a low, thin strip of rail on the shoulder.

When we hit the rail, it immediately began to give. Sparks flew up and blew past the side window in front of my nose as the metal bent outward. Directly below me, on the Eisenhower, I could see the cars I was going to land on. The overpass was high enough for the impact of the fall to kill us just before the traffic hit us and killed us again.

We scraped along the rail; it bent and buckled and screamed. I didn't say anything. All there was time to think was, This is it. The sparks flew upward, left to right.

Just as we were going over—it seemed like we were already gone and falling—we somehow hit a patch of honest shoulder and Harry got some purchase. With it, he managed to wrench the car off the rail and back onto the overpass. The El Dorado curved to the left and cruised down onto the expressway. We drove on to the western suburbs, speechless.

Everybody who drives has a close one now and then, but that one was special. That one was like a cartoon where the character walks out past the cliff edge, sees there's nothing below him, turns and manages to get back to the cliff. We were over the edge and then we weren't. We should have died, but we didn't. We were given bonus time.

I always gave Harry full credit for the save, but he gave it to another power. He had a mystical feeling about it. He believed we'd been preserved so he could perform some exceptional feat.

Now, at my desk in the office, I found myself thinking that he had, after all, started *Who's Hot/Who's Not* and gotten it rolling.

Maybe that was the exceptional feat. Maybe his bonus time was up.

But then I thought, No, that can't be it. The magazine just isn't that good.

TWO

When I got home to Laguna Beach after work I decided I had some responsibilities as the Where Did They Go man. I called Scoop Troop, a little local outfit that walks dogs for people who are leaving town and don't want to abandon their animal to a kennel. Whenever Harry took a trip he engaged them to come over to his castle every day and walk his Samoyed, Savage.

They said he hadn't called. I didn't like that. Harry wouldn't have gone away without making arrangements for Savage. His housekeepers were still around to feed the dog, but I knew that wouldn't be enough maintenance in Harry's opinion.

He loved his Savage as much as I loved my Sashi, and we used to run into each other sometimes at night, with our pets and our plastic bags. A man is at his least dashing when he's picking up after his dog. "Bagging dog doo," Harry said on one such occasion, "is the opposite of Zorro." But he was devoted. He didn't delegate his duties. And when the fire came down the canyon in October of 1993 and everyone was supposed to evacuate, Harry wouldn't go because he couldn't find Savage.

Laguna Beach is a hilly little coastal resort town between Los Angeles and San Diego. It's got several beaches, lots of galleries and restaurants, a couple arts festivals in the summer, and all in all it's beautiful, kind of like Carmel up north. Most of the towns in southern California sprawl out so much you have to drive wherever you go, but you can walk around in Laguna. The town's only real drawback is a susceptibility to disasters. I'd lived there for seven years and in that time we'd had floods, mud slides, smallish earthquakes and one catastrophic fire.

Joanne Shaw and I were still living together when the fire came down Laguna Canyon. On that afternoon we had her four cats plus Sashi in the car as we drove up to Harry's castle to see if he needed any help getting out. The fire had started four miles inland, and the Santa Ana winds, which kick up a few times a year and bend all the trees for a day or two, had whipped it up and driven it down the canyon road toward town. It would eventually destroy more than three hundred homes.

Harry lived in what's called the Top of the World neighborhood, on a hill rising high above the downtown area, looking out to Catalina. The summit of the hill is about half a mile square; there's an elementary school up there, and a park, a few streets with nice houses on them.

Harry stood in the street as we pulled up beside him. I assumed he was worried about his castle. He'd only had it for a year or two, and he was always talking about it, and trying to furnish it, or heat it. The castle took up 18,000 square feet. It had wings. It had a bell tower. He said when he first took possession, "It's like moving your furniture into your high school." The castle was one of the reasons Yasmine left him. He had expected her to keep it nice.

On this day, he was standing in his T-shirt and shorts, looking for Savage, while people drove by with their jewelry and photograph albums.

"I can't figure out his thinking," he said.

The smoke from the houses already destroyed on the north end of town made a huge thundercloud behind him. Harry's face was sweaty and his glasses were smudgy. It was one of the only times I'd ever seen him when he didn't seem confident.

"It's gonna come up the hill, Harry," I warned him.

"If I can't find him by the time it reaches the house I'll go," he said. He squinted down the road. "Do you think he headed down to the water?"

Harry thought his dog was brighter than other dogs. He used to invent brilliant motives for Savage's behavior. He did the same thing with people he liked. He often credited me with subtleties of thought that had never occurred to me.

We left him standing in the street that day and joined the caravan of Lagunans driving south on the Pacific Coast Highway. I didn't see him again until that night, when I came back. Joanne and I had called home to see if the phone had melted, and it had rung. The firefighters had somehow saved the downtown area, and most of the houses on the hill were intact. When I got back, ash had settled on everything in town, but my old rental on Wilson Terrace was still there. I walked through it, relieved. I loved the place. I rented it from an old woman who lived in Oregon and didn't know she could have charged twice as much for it.

I'd just completed my tour when Harry Poe appeared on the front porch, with Savage on a leash.

They were both grinning. Savage looked dirty but healthy. Harry's face and clothes were covered with smudge. His teeth seemed extra white, and his glasses were gone. He was exhilarated.

"You know what he did? You know where he was? In the laundry room," he said proudly. "He'd wet on some towels and pushed them under the door."

Harry wouldn't just leave town without making arrangements. He thought the world of that dog.

• • •

After calling Scoop Troop I walked and fed Sashi. Then I put a frozen dinner in the oven and turned on a *Home Improvement* rerun. I was able to enjoy the "Tool Time" sequences, but the domestic scenes still caused discomfort.

Since Joanne moved out I'd had trouble watching TV. There were well over seventy channels and all but one or two reminded me of her. I couldn't watch shows we'd watched together, or anything with a sexual content or subtext; they made me miss our good times. I'd tried watching just Japanese and Spanish channels, but the sex came through. I couldn't even watch harmless old sitcoms like *The Addams Family,* because Gomez and Morticia had this rapport. About the only programs I could enjoy were bleak stories in which some hopeless misfit came to a bad end. They made me feel better by comparison. There weren't too many of those, though. I would have been grateful for a Samuel Beckett Channel.

I missed Joanne. I kept going over it. We'd always enjoyed each other's company until she moved in. Then we found we had some differences.

Morning energy vs. evening energy, light on vs. light out, meat vs. vegetables, old movies vs. newsmagazines, talk radio vs. music, and then the *kinds* of music. Lots of friends vs. just a few friends. Indoors vs. outdoors. Window open, window closed. Cats, dogs. And then, general outlook.

Joanne had uncovered a few celebrity skeletons in her early career at *Who's Hot* and now she seemed to think everyone was living a lie. This attitude helped her in her work; she could spot a toupee, for instance, faster than anybody. But she couldn't accept anything in a straightforward way. Things aren't always what they seem, but Joanne thought things are *never* what they seem.

Well, here: She thought the late Orville Redenbacher was an actor. Even after his death, she believed that the man we'd seen in the commercials had nothing to do with popcorn, that Orville had been a sham, a character no more real than the Pillsbury doughboy. I couldn't convince her otherwise. I offered to call the company but she said they had to lie. She had reverse gullibility. She was so determined to be a skeptic that she ended up believing all kinds of unlikely things.

We also disagreed about the direction we should be going in at work. Joanne was eager for both of us to move up. She wanted success for herself and whoever she was with. She didn't like it when I asked Harry to take me off Who's Not and put me on Where Did They Go and the little Comeback section at the end. She felt I was smothering my career.

But I think you have to be a young man to do Who's Not.

I'd been in that section for over ten years. That's a lot of bad news. I mean, I covered the decline in popularity of every major media figure who *did* decline in popularity during those years. Over time it made a little rip in my spirit, I think. I got what Harry called "gloat remorse."

Joanne lost all hope for me when I told her I didn't want to work on the Who's Hot section either. I felt it was too gushy. The wild veer in tone after all those years of Who's Not would have given me the bends. I was more comfortable with the contemplative, longer view we took in Where Did They Go. "The one unnecessary section in the book," Joanne called it.

After a while we decided to go back to working together, living apart, and seeing each other now and then. So she moved out, and in two *seconds* she was seeing this guy Ted Fairbanks who worked on the TV end. When I'd told her she should trust people more, I didn't mean him.

Fairbanks was a former NFL quarterback who dressed in this ambitious, pushy, power-hungry way. I never would have gone for him.

Joanne and I had an argument about it right after they started up together. She was telling Neil Purkey in the office about all the "character" Ted Fairbanks had in his face.

"Ted says everything you do in your life shows in your face," she said.

"That's everything you *drink*," I said.

She turned on me. "Ted has character in his face," she said.

"And I suppose I don't," I said.

"That's right, you don't. Because you've never done anything to put it there."

I was hurt. When Joanne and I were living together and irritating each other, I had thought I'd be happier if she left. But after she hooked up with Fairbanks, I couldn't reconstruct my earlier reasoning. Seeing her every day was tough. And I couldn't go over to the Bum's Rush anymore because she and Ted were likely to turn up there. It was the laughter, more than anything. She seemed to laugh all day. Joanne had a big smile. When she and Fairbanks were together, both smiling, it was teeth ahoy.

When Harry noticed me suffering, he was actively sympathetic.

"Want me to fire her?" he offered.

I was shocked. Joanne was only associate managing editor— above her in editorial there was a managing editor, associate editor, executive editor and editor, and they all answered to Harry, the editor-in-chief—but she had a fine instinctive cover sense which he had often acknowledged. She was articulate and attractive. I thought she'd wind up coanchoring the TV version someday. Harry's offer to fire her was a touching and chilling gesture. I said no, of course.

"Fire *him*," I said.

He didn't do it, though. We both thought I was kidding.

By the time Harry disappeared I was doing a little better, I thought. I could get through work by day and some of *Home Improvement* at night. All my stuff was back where I wanted it to be. I was talking to myself easily and freely as I moved through the apartment.

Talking to myself helped. I'm sure there are ways of doing it that aren't healthy—yelling and screaming to yourself, for example, or repeating yourself endlessly—but by and large, I found it a comfort and an aid to thought.

Still, when the doorbell rang that night, I hoped it was Joanne.

I was willing to give her another chance. Sashi and I went to the door expectantly.

It was Harry Poe—smiling, unshaven, wearing a local arts festival sweatshirt and pushing Carole Spangler at me.

"Go on," he told her. "Joe won't mind."

I stared at them. Carole looked pretty much as she had before, although now she had a baseball cap on. She allowed herself to be herded into my living room. Harry followed her, closing the screen door. Then he beamed down at me.

"Hi, Slick," he said. He passed me and moved on into the living room. Sashi gamboled around the woman, enjoying the smell. Sashi lives for company. She thinks all humans are wonderful.

Carole Spangler ignored her, peering critically at my bookcases and furniture.

"We need a place for Carole to stay for an hour or two," Harry explained. "She's got this old boyfriend who has some control issues. What was his name again, hon—Leatherface?"

"Reuben," said Carole shortly.

"I thought I'd drop her somewhere he's never heard of," Harry finished.

I stared at Carole, who glared back at me.

"If you don't want me here say so," she said.

"C'mon, he doesn't mind," Harry said. "It's not like he's in the middle of anything. The only thing is, he doesn't have any wine."

Carole switched the glare to him.

"You're trying to detox me," she said, and started for the door.

"No, no, no, no," said Harry, working around to keep in front of her. "It's no reflection on you. I picked him because he lives here in town. C'mon. Hey. I'll only be gone a few minutes. I'll get your duffel and come right back."

Carole looked at me without enthusiasm.

"He can go to the store," she said, waiting for agreement.

"Sure," said Harry.

"Harry?" I said. " 'Scuse us," I added to Carole.

I preceded him into the kitchen. He kept looking out to make sure Carole wasn't leaving while we talked.

"Everybody thinks you're dead," I told him.

"I'm not. I just had to work something out here. She's got this boyfriend."

"Well, how is that your concern?"

He smiled ruefully, boyishly, and looked back at her.

"I'll admit it. She's got me on the ropes."

I stared into the living room. Carole Spangler was holding one of my books, moving it up close to her face and then back out to arm's length, trying to bring it into focus.

"You don't see it because you don't know her yet. But she's got something. She's got this kind of . . . I don't know . . . fire." Harry shook his head. "It's like all the babes I wasted time with were made of package filler. But she's got substance. You know, she has an interesting history. Her downfall was that she relied on a stranger. Now she's lost faith in men."

" 'Cept maybe the Gallo Brothers." I felt guilty about saying it even before Harry's face went chilly.

"See if you can find something nonalcoholic she might drink," he suggested.

I checked the refrigerator and the pantry while he gazed out at her.

"Substance," he said. "In the jeep on the way back down here the other day, I offered her some extra money. I said, 'I took up a day of your life, how much is it worth?' She thinks it over. Then she opens the glove box and finds a pen, and she says, 'Here, let me total it up on your face.' She had that pen right in my eyes, we were all over the road. She's a dynamo," he finished, looking at her with affectionate concern, "even though she's completely un- dermined her system."

"I've got Diet Pepsi, water and tomato juice," I said.

Harry called into the living room, "How about some Diet Pepsi?"

That got her started for the door again. Harry caught her and they argued about who was going to get the wine and who was going to get the duffel. Carole had left a duffel somewhere and wanted to return for it; Harry didn't want her to go. It was finally agreed that Harry would go get both, because he had the vehicle and the money. Carole subsided into a moody heap on the couch.

Harry gestured for me to follow him, and we went out onto my little porch. It was a clear, temperate night. He shut the screen behind us and looked back through it at Carole.

"I just need to put her on the sidelines while I make a quick run back to the cave," he explained.

I nodded, taking that one in.

"Cave?"

"She and Reuben keep their stuff under a ledge in the hills, up the canyon a ways," he explained. "They've got stuff. Crackers, blankets. Booze. That's why she's disappointed in your setup."

"Well, I don't blame her," I said stiffly. "Maybe she'd rather go back where everything's, you know, just right."

"Now don't suggest that to her," Harry said with some urgency. "I don't want her going back there." He looked at her through the screen. "It's weird how it hits you, isn't it? Unpredictable. There's no accounting . . . For instance, I could never understand what you saw in Joanne. To me, she always seemed abrasive. But here I am, and there's Carole in there. Go figure."

I was willing to agree that it was odd. To me, Carole Spangler was a natural for our weekly What Does He See in Her? section. I mean, you should have seen Harry's ex-wives. I knew them both. They were two different glowing dreams. And they weren't just beautiful; they were charming. Bianca was a little goofy, but in a very sweet way; neither of them was a dummy. I used to look forward to seeing both of them. To me they were the greatest argument in the world for becoming a big shot.

And now here he was, marble-eyed over a woman who looked and acted like a vicious little pirate.

I thought he needed a reminder of his responsibilities.

"Harry, you kinda left the shop door open," I told him. "We've been hearing from Seagal's eagles, and Disney. Everybody wants immediate retractions as usual, and Eden isn't authorized to respond. She's ticked about that. If you're not going to delegate, you should be there."

Harry half-sat on the porch railing, looked up at the sky and scratched his neck.

"Last couple days I've been thinking about that," he said. "Lately I've been losing my edge. About *Who's Hot,* I mean. It's like . . . I did it. You know? I built it up from nothing, and we went to TV, and now here I am. I'm done."

"Harry, we're never done. We start over every Tuesday."

"I mean I accomplished what I set out to do. All I can do now is keep doing it." He looked out at the street. "It's time to do something of value. I realized it yesterday. Last few days I've been hangin' out with the guys who live on the beach, sleep in the canyon. I've been with Carole a lot . . . and yesterday, it hit me: I was meant to meet her. It's all been a direct line. Listen."

He leaned forward, and spoke slowly, distinctly: "On-ramp to on-ramp."

His eyes shone triumphantly through his glasses. I gazed at him for a moment, then shook my head.

"That's not really a thought, Harry."

"No, listen: This is what the bonus time was for. Don't you get it? I was saved on our on-ramp back in Chicago so I could meet Carole on this one. I got it yesterday. The pivotal events of my life: ramp to ramp. I was meant to brake for that woman."

While I stared at him, Carole called out from the living room.

"I coulda been out and back twice by now!"

"On my way!" said Harry, and turned back to me. "Don't worry, Reuben never heard of you. He won't look for her here. See, the thing is"—he bent forward to confide in me—"I can't leave her at the castle because I don't have all the windows hooked up to the security system. You can't believe how much it would cost. And I can't leave her in a hotel because I'm afraid she'd take off. She's impulsive. So I just need you to keep her company for, like, three sitcoms. Just long enough for me to run back to the cave, get her duffel, then go get the wine. And then I'll take her off your hands. You can't possibly mind. I remember you made that big speech about domestic abuse."

During one of the Simpson trials I had remarked, in Harry's presence, that it was cowardly to strike a woman, or at least a weaker woman. This was my big speech.

"The guy beats her?" I asked.

"I'm sure he does."

"You've seen him do it? She says he does?"

"No, but I heard him say he'd kill her if she left him. Right there in the cave. See, I said, 'She's not living here anymore, she's gonna trade up.' So Reuben said he'd kill us both, and I said, 'Well, you better get started 'cause we're going.' So he and I pushed each other around a little bit, and he rolled down the hill and we left. But her duffel's still there. She doesn't have that much stuff, so naturally she wants her duffel."

"What are you gonna say to Reuben?"

"He probably won't even be there. He's probably out looking for us. You can watch her, right?"

I exhaled and jammed my hands in my pockets. I had no excuse to turn him down. He was correct; I didn't have anything better to do.

"Just don't let her leave," he said, "and I'll be right back. Get to know her. I want you to like her, Joe."

She was up from the couch and on her way to the door, glowering at us.

"I'm gone," said Harry. He left the porch and hustled to his jeep.

"Hey!" I called after him. "You better hurry back."

"Goddamn it," added Carole, coming through the door.

He waved and drove off. Carole Spangler and I stared at each other.

"Diet Pepsi," she sneered.

THREE

Carole Spangler and I said nothing further to each other for about thirty seconds. I was the first to get uncomfortable.

"What about food?" I asked. "Ever try any of that?"

We went back into the house. I hadn't been expecting guests, but as it happened the place looked good. I had recently stacked the magazines and taken the laundry to the Laundromat.

She now gave my home a thorough inspection. She checked all the shelves. She walked into the bedroom and looked at my dresser and the books on my bedside table. Had she opened a drawer I would've put up a fight, but she didn't.

I don't own property, exactly, but I do have stuff, and it made me uneasy to watch this woman examining it. Most of it isn't worth anything; you could tell from her reaction. Still, her eyes widened a bit when she saw my four coins. I've got four gold coins in a plastic case; I inherited them from my aunt. One is a $20 piece from 1908. They're supposed to be worth like $1,600 for the whole four.

"You shouldn't have these out," she said.

"They're not exactly out," I replied. "They're here in my bedroom."

"I know a guy who'd kill you for these," she said.

"Well, in that case, they're chocolate inside."

We stared at each other. Then she went back out to the living room and the bookshelves.

"You don't have any books on personal finance," she noted. "You should."

We heard a vehicle. She went to the front window and stared out at my neighbor, Ginny DeVoe, as she came home from somewhere.

"Get a load of her," muttered Carole. "Backs into her driveway like the queen bee." She looked up and down the street.

"Lemme ask you something," she said, her back to me. "If he says he'll bring back wine, will he bring back wine, or some story?"

"I'll ask you one: If he goes back to your cave and that other guy is there, will there be a big confrontation?"

She snorted.

"Don't get your hopes up; they can't fight. They both push and then one of them slips and that's it."

She turned from the window, found a stack of old issues of *Who's Hot/Who's Not* on a bottom shelf and sat on the floor, crossing her legs, to look through a few.

She didn't look as bad as she had the day I met her. She wasn't as drunk, for one thing. Her eyes were clearer and she moved with more assurance. She was surly, but then she'd been living outside. If I had to live outside my attitude would be atrocious. I never even liked to camp out.

"So you and Harry have hit it off," I said finally.

"He's full of ideas," she said, and put the magazines back. Then she stood up, without creaking, and found a jar of change on an upper shelf.

"Lemme take a couple bucks out of here, okay? I want to go to Bay Liquor."

"I thought you were gonna wait."

"Oh, I don't sit, or stay, or report, or any of that," she said mildly.

"But he's bringing your duffel, isn't he?"

"I can pick that up later. There's nothing I've got I can't do without." She picked through the coins. "You'll never roll up these pennies." She stopped and looked back at me.

"I don't know *what* the hell I'm gonna do with them," I said.

She reached in for a handful of change and began sorting it on the shelf. "I'll walk your dog to the store."

"No, that's okay."

"I really only need about a dollar," she said. "I've got some."

I went over and watched while she counted.

"Take a couple quarters anyway—they won't like those pennies at the store," I said.

She swiftly slid two quarters over into her pile.

"Thank you," she said, surprising me.

"Why don't you wait for Harry?" I asked her.

"Because I don't have to." She concentrated on counting for a moment, then added, "Your boss thinks everybody has to go along." She put the coins in her pants pocket. "I thought he was going to buy some wine, but now I think he's an evangelist."

She took the money and walked to the door. I went with her.

"Harry thinks this Reuben might get you if you go out," I said.

She laughed. Her whole face exploded, in a big wide grin.

"Reuben won't hurt me," she said. "Reuben won't even contradict me."

"Didn't he say he'd kill you? Doesn't he hit you?"

She brought it down to a kind of indulgent smile.

"He goes like this," she said, and raised her hands to her head as if warding off punches.

· · ·

After she left, I called Eden Ramos, our head of sales, at her home to tell her Harry was alive. Eden had been running the office while Harry was missing, and although she'd been clearly distressed, she'd also begun thinking of herself as the new boss. She'd been calling people into her office to discuss their roles. She needed to get the news before she got too involved in restructuring everything.

Harry's return meant I had to address a neglected task of my own: I had to get back to work on our millennium issue. Harry wanted our millennium issue to compare favorably with everyone else's millennium issue. We were going to have a Future Hot list, and a Future Not list, and to kiss off the twentieth century, Harry had chosen me to pick the ninety-nine hottest celebrities of the last hundred years. That is, the ninety-nine performers who had driven the public into the biggest frenzy.

Harry's lists were always divisible by 9. He felt Top Ten and Hundred lists were clichéd and arbitrary, and 9 was his lucky number. His birthday was April 9th. He liked to have big meetings on the 9th. He and I escaped death in the car in Chicago on December 18th. So his lists in the magazine were always the 9 Biggest Star Tantrums of the Year or the 18 Best Cosmetic Surgeries. At first people had considered it a pointless conceit on Harry's part, but it had evolved into a nice signature for him and now he was known for it. Readers would have been disappointed if we'd ever done a list that couldn't break down to 9.

Harry had tabbed me to review the century because he felt I had more perspective than the rest of the staff. "You're the only one who knows anything about the first fifty years," he'd said.

So it was up to me to come up with a strong group. Harry didn't want anyone helping me—especially not readers. Harry had nothing but contempt for magazines like *Time,* which had accepted input from its readership for its list. He didn't think professionals should solicit amateur assistance.

I was trying to shorten my master list when Harry returned,

dirty and disheveled. His shoes and cuffs were muddy; so was the seat of his pants. He dropped an old beige canvas bag on the floor as he came into the living room. When he heard Carole Spangler was gone, he went all Jack Palance.

"You let her go out for wine?" he asked me softly.

"She didn't say for sure she was gonna buy wine. Maybe she wanted a Slurpee."

"I asked you to keep her here."

"What was I gonna do, tackle her?"

"She was supposed to wait for me."

"Well, she weighed you against Bay Liquor and Bay Liquor won."

"You couldn't hold her ten minutes? What did you do, kick her out? Did you even TRY?"

"Goddamn it, Harry, it was up to her."

"You know I almost died out there, getting that," he informed me, toeing the bag on the floor.

"Problem with Reuben?"

Harry stared at Sashi, breathing heavily through his nose.

"I drove as far off the road as I could, and then I started climbing. They sleep in this little—it's like an eye socket in this big boulder in the hills. It was dark. I had a flashlight. I kept slipping because it's steep." He held his palm up to show me the angle. "So I slid back once and dropped the flash. Crawled back up to where it was. Picked it up. Turned it on. And right in my face, right in the beam, two feet away, looking at me . . ." He shivered, picturing it.

"What?" I asked.

"Possum," he said shortly.

We were silent a moment, each of us picturing a possum.

"*God,* they're homely," said Harry. "Beady eyes. Fat and skittery. Right in my face like that . . . It was like, the first thing you'd see if you went to hell. So I jumped—which, when you consider I was lying on my stomach, that's noteworthy. And I slid back down the hill. Dropped the flash again . . . and then I had to go back up anyway, and find the cave, and get this"—he kicked it—"bag. And all the time that thing was there somewhere, in the dark, with its little . . ." He curled his upper lip to show his teeth. "I CALLED for Reuben. I'da been delighted to see Reuben. He wasn't there. I *guess* it was a possum. It was either a possum or a record-breaking rat."

"So that's her duffel?"

"Yeah." He looked down at it moodily. "That's it. Good thing I saved it. No telling what might have happened if all the dirty clothes got in the wrong hands."

"You looked in the bag?"

"You're goddamn right." He brought it over to the coffee table. He unzipped it and I looked in.

"It's clothes," I assented.

"Mostly. There's also a toy gun, like a *Star Trek* gun." He pushed some clothes aside and came up with a sleek little gray metallic oddity, a kind of combination of a phaser and a Pez dispenser. You apparently slid back a tab on top of the barrel and pressed a button on the grip and it was supposed to do something, but it didn't. Harry showed me.

"This is her stuff," I said to him.

"Oh, so I shouldn't have opened it. What would you have done?"

"I would have done everything just the same as you except I never would have picked her up in the first place."

"I don't care," said Harry, zipping the duffel back up. "Everything that's happened to me since I met her—even the possum—has been vivid and unique. I am embarking on something."

"Do you know she doesn't like you?"

"Of course I do," he said impatiently. "That's not unprecedented. Yasmine couldn't stand me at first. And she couldn't stand me at the end, but in between, I won her over. Carole thinks I'm insensitive. But I can temper that. I feel something intense and powerful when I'm with her. Ever hear of it?"

"Sure, Harry."

"You said Bay Liquor." He started out.

"You should stop by the police station and tell 'em you're still alive," I called after him.

I went back to the Hot 99 list. I was wrestling with Shirley Temple when Harry returned a half hour later, his disposition unimproved.

"She's not at Bay Liquor, she's not between here and Bay Liquor, and the cops haven't seen her. I'm holding you responsible."

I thought Carole Spangler was more than tough enough to spend a night out on her own. And Harry's attitude irked me.

"Well, thanks all to hell for bringing her over," I said.

"And thanks all to hell for letting her leave."

"I'm gonna let you leave too, Harry."

He glared at me. Then he picked up Carole Spangler's duffel, turned stiffly and walked over to Sashi. He bent over and passed the duffel under her nose. She showed polite curiosity. He unzipped the bag and treated her to the smell of an old sweatshirt. She seemed disappointed.

"She doesn't get it," I told him. "She's not a bloodhound. She's a barge dog."

Harry gave up and went to the door.

"You should go look for her yourself," he said on the way out. " 'Cause if we don't find her, you won't have to worry about the Hot 99."

I went out to the porch and hollered at him as he got in his car.

"I didn't want to do the Hot 99 anyway! I wanted to do the *Shoulda*-Been-Hot 99! The Unjustly Neglected 99! Something original!"

He waved me off irritably as he drove away. He always hated that idea.

• • •

As it happened, I did find Carole Spangler. But not until the following morning, on the side of the road.

I had had trouble sleeping, so I was running late. I had been bedding down on the couch, lately, to old videos, turned down low. That night I'd remained awake despite the help of one of my most reliable movies, *North by Northwest*. I still missed Joanne. It bothered me that Eva Marie Saint was drooling over Cary Grant. I only got about four hours of sleep, and I woke up cranky. My eyes hurt. I had to race through my shower.

Harry always said he only needed four hours' sleep a night. He never seemed tired. I envied him this quality.

Laguna Canyon Road is a tricky stretch, winding about eight miles inland from town before it reaches the 405 freeway. It's dangerous because it's snaky and because there's two-way traffic. I drove it pretty fast that morning. I wasn't as cautious as I used to be.

I sped through the canyon, past cattle, the remnants of the old Irvine Ranch herd, and came up on the 405. Beside the north on-ramp stood Carole Spangler, with a big hand-printed sign. I slowed, pulled over and stopped beyond her, on the dusty shoulder.

The sign said, "Gotta GET THERE FAST? Use a CARPOOL COMPANION!" In smaller lettering, below, it said, "Carpool Lane" and "$30."

She had found herself a clean, oversized navy blue sweatshirt and washed her hair somewhere. She had a shopping bag on the ground beside her. Her pants and sneakers were the same as she'd had on the night before. As I got out of my car and walked up to her, she started toward me. When she recognized me, she stopped and turned around once, a little kind of twirl.

"How does it work?" I asked.

"How do you think? I go up north with the driver, turn the sign around and come back with somebody else." She showed me

the back of the sign, which read the same except that the word
"there" had been replaced by the word "home."

"Your boss gave me the idea," she said, "by being such a shit."

I squinted at the passing traffic.

"It's a little dangerous. . . . You might get picked up by an even
bigger one."

"I'll be fine. These people . . . they're all going to work. Some
of them are really late. They need the carpool lane. They won't
pick me up today, maybe. But they'll see the sign. And the *next*
time they're late, they'll pick me up. They might even pick Reuben
up."

"Reuben's doing this too?" Cars passed us, the drivers staring
at her sign as they curved onto the northgoing ramp.

"Reuben's on the on-ramp to the 5," she said, pointing up
ahead. That ramp, the one to the Santa Ana Freeway, was about
a mile farther up the canyon road.

"With the same kinda sign?"

"We're a company," she said.

"Well," I said, watching the cars go by, "I'm a little late today
myself. I'll be your first customer."

She peered at me.

"You're not, like, just taking me to Harry Poe."

"No," I said, surprised. "I didn't think of that."

"Okay. Thirty bucks."

· · ·

I slid over to the carpool lane and we sailed past the jammed-up
commuters on the 405. Carole Spangler looked out her window.

"See, now I'm saving you a lot of time," she said. "And time
is money." She glanced at me. "You think I should charge more
than thirty?"

I thought it over.

"Nah," I said finally. "Too much more, they'll think there's
something else included. Or they'll decide it's too expensive and

just take a chance on the fine." I gestured at the sign as we went beneath it—it said the fine for using the carpool lane illegally was $271.

"I can do this all day," she said. "There's always people in a hurry. Going north and south."

Well, of course it was a mockery of the whole carpool lane concept. It was probably illegal, or soon would be if somebody noticed what she was doing. On the other hand, you had to applaud her resourcefulness. She'd turned insult into inspiration.

She looked at the cars to our right as we went north. They were all at a standstill.

"Now isn't this nice?" she asked me earnestly. "You're sticking it to every one of these people."

"I'm starting to see why Harry likes you," I said.

She was rocking a bit in the passenger seat, forward and back. Kind of like a jockey, riding the car forward. She had a lot of intensity. In a hurry to get on to the next ride.

"He came by with your duffel last night but you were gone," I went on. "He was upset."

"Where's the duffel now?"

"He's got it."

"Tell him to give it to you, and I'll come pick it up."

I hesitated, then let curiosity win out.

"He, uh, took a look in it. I guess there's a toy gun in there."

"You guess?"

"Well, yeah. I mean, I saw it. He saw it, I saw it." I drove on a little farther. "I was just curious, you know, where you got it. Why you had it. Never mind."

After a moment, she said, "It's a Facer."

"That's what we thought. From an old *Star Trek* game or something, huh."

"Not a phaser. A Facer." She put her feet up on the dashboard. "My ex-husband's name is Kevin Face, and he invented that weapon. It took the country by storm."

Even with the carpool lane, we had some time before us as we went up through Huntington Beach, Long Beach and Manhattan Beach. The sense of well-being that comes from zooming by a bunch of fellow drivers seemed to loosen Carole up. She told me most of her story that day, on the way up to the office. I heard the rest later, in dribs and drabs, from Harry mostly, but I'll encapsulate here.

Carole Spangler had had money, briefly. "My father was the dentist to the stars," she said. He capped the teeth of many fine performers. He and her mother, a former actress, had died in a crash on Laguna Canyon Road, coming home from a party up north. Carole, their only daughter, had been left at twenty-three with $700,000.

Kevin Face was new to her. He'd come in recently from the East Coast and lived in Newport Beach, just up the coast highway. He was a promoter, and an inventor, kind of. He had an idea for a special self-defense weapon to be used by women and children. Carole met him at a friend's party. They got married four months after her parents' death.

Face made a corporation out of his weapon idea, which he called the Facer. It was supposed to be a kind of mild laser. He got the idea from *Star Trek*—"Him and everybody else," she said. Kevin was undaunted by the fact that others were developing self-defense weapons for women at the same time; he was confident that his model would win out. He formed a company and issued stock certificates to anyone who'd help finance prototypes, testing, offices in Newport Beach and a promotional video.

Development cost more than expected, however, and the Facer turned out to be prohibitively potent.

"He couldn't legalize it," she said. "I mean, the way the thing worked, private citizens would never be allowed to use it. I'm not sure soldiers would be allowed to use it. He couldn't bring it under control. If I had one, working, in my hand, I could put your eye out. I could put your eye OUT."

Expenses piled up while Kevin tried to work out the bugs in his product.

"He got money from his father, his friends and their friends. He even got a couple Hollywood idiots to go in on it. But he had to pay patent fees and development money and overhead on the offices. Finally he said 'we' had to put a little of 'our' money in, just to get over the top. We were just this side of getting over the top. Well, there it was. I never said, 'Whaddya mean, *our* money?' I listened to my heart. I stood by my man. I watched the promotional video. And with that money, we went back into R & D, and we refined the Facer. And we tested it. One of the testers got a hole right through his hand. And to this day, no one has bought the damn thing. Nobody was ever ALLOWED to buy it. It never even got on the shelf. I saved one that didn't work. The ones that worked were too dangerous to even pick up. If you shot it into the ground you'd kill somebody in Beijing. I finally told him he should go out in the desert and use one on himself. I keep that one in my duffel, for a souvenir. A reminder.

"I didn't do it for nothing, though. He made me a board member. I was on the board, so I got tangled up in his debts. Kevin didn't lose much, because he was using everybody else's money. I got a stock certificate. I kept it until I moved into the cave with Reuben. Then one night I ran out of leaves."

For a while, after they had lost their house, she and Face had lived in an apartment together. He mostly stayed away, and finally he left altogether. She couldn't stand him, but she didn't want him to leave. "I missed him when he left," she said. "I wasn't done with him yet. I had some further things to say to him."

She told this story in a calm, casual tone except for occasional phrases where she would suddenly get back in the moment: "I was willing to go along and make the best of the situation the *pissant* got me into, but he couldn't even face it himself. I wrote on the mirror in lipstick, you know, FUCK YOU, but I don't think he ever saw it. He wouldn't look at himself. So how could he see it?"

She blamed herself for losing the money, for losing her house. After Kevin left, she drank nonstop and behaved promiscuously. "I went home with a married man whose wife was away for the weekend. Passed out and peed on his mattress. He said, 'How am I gonna explain this?' "

Eventually she had found a spot on the bottom of the heap with Reuben, in the cave, with no mattress to worry about. "I like Reuben," she said, "because he's not an entrepreneur."

We rode on silently for a while after she finished this story.

"I never had anything like that happen to me," I offered after a bit, "but I know what it's like to regret, you know, something. When I was in college, I did something I've always felt bad about. In fact I got kicked out because of it. I don't even know why I did it. I look back now and I can't even—"

"Excuse me?" she asked. "You think you can match my story with an 'I didn't graduate' story?"

There was a little pause.

"It made the papers," I muttered finally, a little sullenly.

"Oh, tell it if you want to."

"No, that's all right," I said with dignity.

We got up past LAX and I exited at Wilshire. At the first red light she hopped out of the car with her rolled-up sign and her shopping bag.

"If I'm on this end when you come back down, pull over," she said. "I'll discount you five dollars." She showed me the twenty and the ten before putting them in her pocket. "I already topped the entire lifetime sales on the Facer."

FOUR

I reached the office too late to witness Harry's welcome back from the missing. I heard that most of the department heads hugged him. I don't think there was any hypocrisy in that. The hugs were for Harry's good points.

He looked all settled in at his desk, and he positively beamed when I told him I'd driven Carole Spangler up north, but he clouded up when I added that she'd gotten out on Wilshire.

"You didn't bring her in?"

"She didn't want to come in. She's got a new business."

His eyes got positively buggy as I told him about Carpool Companions. He rose, walked past me, out of his office and out of the building, without another word.

About a half hour later he returned and found me at my desk.

"She wasn't on the corner," he said, standing over me. "She wasn't anywhere on Wilshire."

"Well, she probably got a ride back down south."

He looked at me grimly for a moment.

"Okay," he said finally. "List meeting."

·   ·   ·

Harry herded us into the conference room. Included at this preliminary meeting were Peter Hood, head of the art department; Neil
Purkey and Joanne, who would be compiling the Future Hot list;
and Steve Kluszewski, who oversaw our office computer system
and would be putting the millennium issue highlights on our website.

If Jimmy Nations was the office hothead, Steve was our
brooder. He was a big, bald, blue-eyed guy who always seemed to
be simmering. When he first joined us, he had a decent sense of
humor, but lately it hadn't been in evidence. At the Bum's Rush
after work, he had gotten into the habit of bad-mouthing absent
coworkers venomously, beyond the bonds of ordinary bitching, for
no discernible reason. Recently his wife had gotten sick and that
had cranked him up further. He'd been extra touchy lately, like
the guy in the Abbott & Costello routine who becomes irrational
whenever someone mentions the Susquehanna Hat Company. He
was good with our computer system, though. Whenever we
crashed, Steve brought us up.

Peter Hood was slender, with glasses and a red beard and a
patient expression. He had the best posture in the building. He sat
up so straight, with his head so high, that he made a kind of phys-
ical trick out of taking notes. He was precise and thorough, and
almost never showed enthusiasm. The impression he gave was that
whatever the task, he could do it, but it wasn't going to be easy.
Harry would tell him what he wanted in the way of graphics, and
Peter would acquiesce. He would close his eyes and nod. Today
he was coughing and sniffling a bit, seemed to have a cold. Whenever he coughed, Steve Kluszewski, who sat next to him, shot him
a dirty look.

Neil Purkey slouched in his seat beside me. He was tall and
skinny, with curly black hair and a mustache. He'd been at *WH/
WN* almost as long as me, and was tired of it. He wanted to be a
writer. A few years before, he'd cowritten an episode of a one-

season sitcom called *Hyde & Chic,* and although he'd done nothing since, he considered himself and Larry David equals.

Joanne looked great, as usual. She'd recently gotten her hair redone in that sexy fashion that suggests an explosion. On this morning she was businesslike and casual—a little preoccupied, as if she was looking beyond this meeting to another one. That was my interpretation, anyway. She was chewing on a Bic pen.

Harry sat at the head of the table.

"Let's get the century over with," said Harry briskly. "The bonus issue is gonna be promoted as a collectible. It'll have Joe's hottest ninety-nine of the century, plus our Future Hot and Future Not lists. Joanne and Neil, you've got the Future Hots."

This was the kind of remark upon which, over the years, every possible variation had been rung. "I've got the Hots," "She's got the Hots," "Who's got the Hots" . . . no one reacted to it anymore. Except me, thinking about Joanne's Future Hots.

"I'll personally handle the Future Nots," Harry went on. "Today Joe is showing his preliminary hottest ninety-nine so Peter can start on the art, which has to *pulsate.*" Peter's eyes closed, and he nodded. "We also need to hear these names so we know Joe didn't sneak in people like Oscar Levant and L. Q. Jones." Harry looked at me. "Go."

"Okay, I have a list here," I said, "from which will come the final ninety-nine. Before passing it around, I'd like to explain a couple ground rules we began with. One, we're an entertainment magazine, so no statesmen or physicists or inventors or Gandhi. Also we're Americans—we cover the American scene, so again, no Gandhi. However, I adjusted that second rule. I included several people who weren't born here."

"Why?" demanded Harry.

"Because if I hadn't, I couldn't have considered Valentino, Chaplin, Garbo, Cary Grant or the Beatles."

"Read the list," he said.

"I've got copies right here; I'd rather hand them around."

"No. When I hear the names I can tell if they're appropriate."
He closed his eyes and sat back.

I sighed and looked at my top sheet.

"This isn't the final order," I said. "It's just the order I originally wrote them down in." I cleared my throat. "Elvis. Marilyn.
Babe Ruth. Muhammad Ali. Valentino, Chaplin, Garbo, Sinatra.
Clark Gable. John Wayne. Shirley Temple. Michael Jordan. Al Jol-
son—"

I heard a snort from Neil Purkey, but continued.

"Charles Lindbergh—"

"Come ON," said Joanne. "You've got Lindbergh before Madonna?"

"Lindbergh was bigger than anybody, twice," I said.

"What about O. J.?" asked Peter Hood.

"He's in a Notorious sidebar with Al Capone," I said. "There's
another sidebar for rock, one for teams, like Martin & Lewis and
Sonny & Cher, and two sidebars for television, one for leading
players and one for supporting players." I consulted my pages.
"That one has Rochester, Barney Fife, Granny Clampett, Keith
Partridge, Spock, Fonzie and Kramer. I also have a Bottle Rocket
sidebar with Johnnie Ray, Fess Parker and Tiny Tim. Okay, moving back to the master list . . . Madonna. Brando. James
Dean. . . ."

"No," said Harry, speaking for the first time since I'd begun.
"It's wrong."

I stopped reading. We all waited while he took his glasses off
and, holding them out from his face, looked through them.

"We need better people," he said finally.

I stared at him.

"Whaddya mean? Longer legs?"

"No . . . more impressive. Like Einstein."

"Einstein," I repeated stupidly.

"And Freud," said Harry. "And JFK and Jackie. And Di. And
Mother Teresa."

"*Hot?* Mother Teresa?" I was mystified.

"Hey, how about Christ?" said Neil. "He's big in any century."

"What do you mean?" I said, stunned. "We're entertainment only."

"Well, maybe that's a flaw," replied Harry. "You can't have a discussion of an entire century and include the names of Fess Parker and Johnnie Ray."

"They're not on the list," I said patiently. "They're in a side-bar. And no matter how you feel about it, for a minute there, they were both extremely hot."

"Davy Crockett was hot," said Harry. "Not Fess Parker."

Peter Hood coughed, as he'd been doing periodically throughout, and Steve Kluszewski turned on him.

"You've got a cold," Steve said, "but you won't go home. You know why?"

"Because he's tough," said Joanne. "Aren't you, Peter?"

"Because he's inconsiderate," said Steve. "He doesn't care who else gets sick." Steve addressed us all: "I don't know who Johnnie Ray is, and furthermore I don't give a shit. Tell me what to put on the website, I'll do it. Meantime I'd like to get back to work. I need to leave early." He stood up, and his chair fell over behind him. He bent over and righted the chair. "If that's okay," he said, and looked at Harry.

"How's the wife?" Harry asked.

"She went from cold to pneumonia to pleurisy," he said slowly. "She's supposed to recover with the antibiotics."

"Well, why don't you go home, or back to the hospital?"

"Yeah, well, somebody shoulda gone home, or coughed the other way, or it wouldn't've happened."

Whereupon he left.

"Jesus," said Peter Hood. "Like I got a cold to screw him."

"He thinks Claudia got sick because he brought a bug home from work," said Joanne.

"We'll send some more flowers," said Harry. "Does anybody visit?"

"Steve doesn't encourage it," said Neil.

Harry moved on.

"From you, tomorrow," he told me, "a numbered list. One to ninety-nine. And I want some substance to it. Who's Number One going to be? That's where we'll stand or fall." He looked around the table. "Well?"

"How about Christ?" said Neil.

"What is this Christ thing?" I demanded.

"He's a big name."

Harry looked doubtful.

"Christ isn't really identified with this century," he said.

"We got the whole millennium idea from him," said Neil. "Didn't we?"

"He's not an American," said Peter.

"No, but he could get in on Joe's Beatles rule," said Neil.

"John Lennon said the Beatles were bigger than Christ," Harry recalled. "What if we put the Beatles first and Christ second?"

I was reduced to saying, "What?"

"See," Harry told me, "your list is too light. We can't let the whole century boil down to just actors and athletes. You've got to bring out the big guns. Einstein. Gandhi. Freud. Christ."

"We're an entertainment magazine," I said indignantly. "It'd make Einstein and Jesus look like a couple of song-and-dance men."

"Who was the hottest," Harry intoned. "That is your criterion. Put them in order of peak temperature."

"First off," I argued, "the list should be confined to twentieth-century mortals. And secondly, if we include physicists and psychoanalysts and heads of state we're gonna look dumb. We don't belong on that playing field. We're lightweight."

"I'm TIRED of lightweight!" Harry roared, and then glowered at me. "I want some muscle in that list, and I want copy that's dignified, profound, memorable, sexy and funny, depending on the person."

I exhaled, trying to keep my temper.

"You're the one," I reminded him, "who always said 'Entertainment only.'"

"If I want to change my mind, I change it. If I say big picture, you pull back and show it."

"I don't know if I'm your guy," I said.

"I don't either," he replied, getting up. "We'll find out tomorrow."

As he left, I gazed at Neil Purkey, who was leaning back in his chair and stretching.

"'What about Christ? He's big in any century,'" I imitated him, up in my nose.

"Hey," he said, bringing his chair down. "It'll be more fun this way."

"It'll be inane," I insisted. "Beatles, Christ, Marilyn, Einstein, Freud, Gandhi, Madonna, Hitler and Lucy."

"Perfect," said Neil.

I rubbed my forehead. Harry was usually right even when he was wrong.

"You should go with exactly the order you just said," said Neil. "That was fine."

"I don't even know what I said. I was being sarcastic."

"Beatles, then Christ," said Joanne, rising. "Come on, Neil. We've got to figure out the Future Hots."

"Am I the only one who thinks it odd that Harry is suddenly throwing these heavy names around?" I asked.

"No, I agree," said Peter Hood. "It's very strange. It's like he's getting serious."

· · ·

Reuben Schifrin abandoned competitive society because every time he thought of something great, somebody else came out with it immediately. He thought of a TV series about a sports bar, and then they did *Cheers*. He started a screenplay called *Lethal Weapon*—the Mel Gibson picture came out. He started a screenplay called *Lethal Weapon II,* but there again . . . He had been on the verge of inventing a liquid that took sticky label residue off books and CD covers, but then they came out with Goo Gone.

Reuben had lost heart and given in to gravity. He was convinced that no matter what he came up with, it would be staring back at him from a store shelf or a movie marquee the following morning.

I wouldn't have learned this if I hadn't encountered Carole Spangler again, on the way home after work. Too late to use her service; I'd made it all the way down to Laguna Canyon Road. She was walking inland, on the shoulder, toward the coast and town, in the dusk.

I passed her, pulled over and waited, watching in the rearview while she stumped up to the car and got in.

"What a day," she said.

"Lotta rides?"

She shot me a look and then looked back to the road.

"Couple."

"Don't want me to see your roll?"

"The worst thing," she said, ignoring my remark, "is the talk. You have to make it clear that they're buying a passenger, not a real companion. I had to clarify that all day. I had one guy *sing* all the way up, with the Frank Sinatra *Duets* tape. Every word. From now on I'm gonna tell 'em it's twice the price if you open your mouth."

We curled down the canyon road, approaching town and the ocean. About two miles from town there's a particularly snaky section called the Big Bend by natives, which curves to the right and then to the left. As I negotiated it, I was feeling sorry for myself. I knew when I got home I had to number all those celebrities.

"If you were making a list of the hottest people of the century," I asked, "would you include Jesus?"

She didn't answer right away. I thought she was just rejecting the question, but as the road straightened out, she responded.

"No. It's unfair to the other people who actually had to live through this bullshit hundred years."

I drove on, thoughtfully.

"I am *so* glad this century is over," she added.

"Anyway, he shouldn't be *second,*" I decided finally. "He's the kind of guy, should either be first, or not on at all. Okay. He's out. I agree. Inappropriate in this context. Let Harry put him back in. Thanks."

"Pull over up here," she said.

I went onto a narrow shoulder which separated the canyon road from a couple of rocky hills on the right. Vegetation was coming back to cover the stone; when the fire swept down the canyon it denuded all the hills into a bumpy kind of moon surface; it had taken years to grow back this far. There were little ledges and indentations among the rock formations, and Carole said she lived in one of them, with Reuben.

I felt guilty—dropping someone off at their cave.

"Hey," I said as she got out. "Thanks for the input. You helped me out. If you could use a dinner, I guess I owe you one."

"Kay," she said. "Be over a little later."

She started up the grassy incline from the road.

"Well," I called after her, "I didn't exactly mean tonight. I've got to do this list."

She stopped and squinted back at me, a short, sturdy figure in the tall, dry grass.

"Oh," she said.

"But it's okay," I said quickly. "It's okay. I said a dinner, I meant a dinner. You want to come over now?"

"No," she said. "I want to lay down first."

She turned and walked on. I waited for a gap in the homecoming commuter traffic and got back on the road into downtown Laguna.

I bought two Cornish hens at Albertson's because I know how to do those. Looking back, I feel certain that I had omitted Reuben from the dinner invitation, but Carole either didn't hear it that way, or didn't care, because she brought him with her and I was a hen short.

Reuben was tall. Gangly, with a droopy mustache and semi-beard, big brown eyes and a great tan. He kept his head forward and down a little. He had an old windbreaker on, over a shirt or two, and big boots without laces, with their tongues hanging out.

Carole said, "How ya doin'?" I showed them both into the living room, excused myself and went to the bedroom. She followed me, stood in the doorway while I put my coins away, and said, "He's not the one I meant."

I went back out to the living room with her and stood, while she sat on the couch next to Reuben. He was drumming his fingers on the armrest and nodding rhythmically at Sashi, who sniffed his boots.

"She probably smells rat," he said. "I kicked a rat about thirty yards."

"That's probably it then," I agreed. "Were you a carpool companion today?"

"Only once, going up, and I had to wait for the same guy to pick me up coming back," he said. "I don't get picked up like she does. But if we use more women and feebler men we should do okay."

"It was partly Reuben's idea," Carole informed me. "He thought of the name."

"Somebody'll steal it," he said confidently. "Somebody'll make a whole escort service out of it."

"Yeah, me," said Carole. "I'm gonna."

Reuben scanned my shelves, still nodding.

"I see you got a lot of books," he said.

"Reuben wrote a novel about the future and time travel," said Carole, "and then they came out with *Back to the Future*. Everything he ever thought of, right then somebody did it." She added the *Lethal Weapon* and Goo Gone stories.

"I don't even try anymore," he said.

"At least you think of good things," said Carole. "You don't come up with a new formula for gull shit, like most people."

"If I were a good Taoist I wouldn't even care," he said. "But it hurts to be in a bar and see some clown on TV getting rich behind something I thought of."

"Maybe you should do something that's already been done," I suggested.

He stared at me.

"What the hell good is that?" he demanded.

"Well, something traditional, only with your own personal slant on it that nobody could duplicate," I said. "Like for instance, I always thought it would be smart to write a hit Christmas song, or Christmas movie. Then every year, it comes out again, like an annuity. One good Christmas song could support you for a lifetime."

"I think Christmas is a crock of shit," declared Reuben.

"Well, there's your title," I said brightly. "I—"

"What's for dinner?" asked Carole.

What I couldn't figure out, watching them dismantle the birds in my kitchen, was where Harry had gotten the idea that Carole was threatened by this guy. She showed no signs of that kind of tension around him. She was completely self-assured; sort of condescendingly kind to him. She slapped his hand when he reached across. She ate off his plate. She cued him on what stories to tell and then finished the stories for him. She acted in every way like someone in charge.

Two Cornish hens didn't go very far with three of us, and Carole expressed an interest in microwave popcorn as something they didn't get too much of, so I made some. Seeing Orville on the box made me kind of sad. Reuben was in the bathroom and Carole and I were eating the popcorn when Harry arrived.

I'd left the front door unlocked; Harry called my name from the doorway. I called back from the kitchen and he came in, saying something about the Hot 99 list. When he saw Carole sitting at my kitchen table, he stopped so suddenly that I was reminded of when I worked one summer at an insurance claims office back in Chicago.

It was a second-floor office, at the top of a flight of stairs. The entrance door was clear glass, with no lettering on it. My desk was near the door, and my clerical duties were secondary, in my colleagues' view, to my main responsibility of letting them know whenever visitors reached the top of the stairs.

We were a fun-loving crew, and few things are funnier than watching someone walk into a glass door instead of the open doorway he expected to go through. First-timers never seemed to notice the door handle.

No one cracked the glass or got really hurt while I was working there; visitors would always pause momentarily at the top of the stairs to compose themselves before stepping into the "doorway," so they never built up a damaging head of steam. They'd see us all, at our desks, looking up expectantly, and they'd walk right into the glass. Wow. I look back on those shocked faces today and I'm young again. The expressions were always priceless . . . and so was Harry's when he walked into the sight of Carole Spangler in my kitchen.

FIVE

Harry stood in the kitchen doorway, looking from Carole to me to the Cornish hens. He looked Sicilian; operatic. He even folded his arms.

"I see," he said.

"Where's my duffel?" demanded Carole.

Harry focused on me.

"You couldn't keep her here last night," he said, "but you got her here tonight. You couldn't bring her to the office, but you got her into your kitchen."

He looked from the hen remnants to Sashi, who was still hoping for scraps, and then back to me. "The years turn to smoke," he said.

Reuben appeared behind him all at once, tall in the kitchen doorway. Harry saw him peripherally; he flinched and raised his arms involuntarily, like W. C. Fields used to do.

"They're here for dinner, Harry," I said.

Harry blinked a few times while he took this in. Carole snickered at him.

She sat slouched at the table, running her tongue over her teeth and rubbing her hands with a paper towel. I tried looking at her the way Harry and Reuben apparently saw her. Sober, she had hazel eyes. Her face was more tan than red this evening. I thought I could place her age around thirty. She might have had a nice figure, although it was difficult to tell because she always wore big baggy sweatshirts. She didn't seem to rattle easily; that was an attractive quality. Her face was creased a bit, but it wasn't ugly. Once in the car earlier that day, I had glanced over and seen her looking ahead like a pioneer woman, with her chin stuck out.

No, I concluded: I was an idiot to let Joanne get away. All Joanne really wanted was for me to be a little more adventurous. Usually, when a woman criticizes a man she's living with, she's right. Why couldn't we ever admit that?

Harry's first assessment of the situation had been so mistaken that he was still searching for the proper stance. He had covered for a moment by finding a problem with his glasses. Now he put them back on and addressed Carole.

"Joe tells me," he said conversationally, "that you've started a carpool lane escort service."

She didn't seem to think this required a response. Anyway, she didn't respond.

"I think that's brilliant," he went on. "I really mean that. But I don't think you should be out there, accepting rides from just whoever."

Carole barked a laugh.

"It's okay if you throw me in your jeep, but it's not okay if I get in somebody else's," she said.

"It isn't safe. You should delegate it. Build up a workforce of riders, and make it clear to the commuters that they're with your company, and not just hitchhikers or derelicts."

"I already thought of that," said Reuben, as he had probably said so many times before.

"You have to make it clear you're organized," Harry continued.

"Okay," said Carole. "You want to help? Get us uniforms.

Make up uniforms that have 'Carpool Companions' stenciled on
'em. And then bring 'em over in my DUFFEL."

"Well, the duffel's at my place," said Harry. "And that brings
up my other suggestion." He turned his back on Reuben to make
it clear he was addressing Carole only. "Until you find a place with
running water, you should stay at my house. I have an unoccupied,
uh, wing. You'd have a whole section of the building to yourself,
pretty much."

Reuben reacted poorly to this suggestion.

"She's okay where she is," he said.

"She's in a cave," said Harry.

"Hey, up yours," said Reuben. He took a pace toward Harry,
which brought them toe-to-toe. Harry looked up at him, coolly.

"People will say we're in love," he said.

Reuben shoved Harry. Harry bounced back into Reuben's
face.

"Hey! Damnit, grow up," I told them. "You're in my kitchen."

"She's not staying with somebody beats on her," said Harry,
choosing to talk tougher.

Reuben snorted.

"I don't beat her," he said. "But I'll kick *your* ass."

"Harry, I think maybe your picture's fuzzy on this," I said.

"What do you know about it?" he demanded.

"Well, I saw the way they eat dinner."

Harry stared at Carole, who remained at the table, eating popcorn.

"He doesn't hit you?" asked Harry.

She shrugged. "More the other way around."

"Well, then, why'd you leave with me last night?"

"Ran out of wine," she said laconically.

Harry turned to Reuben. "You said you were gonna kill her,"
he said.

Reuben's gaze flickered.

"I'm in a transitional period," he said formally. "From a Western to an Eastern outlook. Sometimes I still talk Western. But I'd never hurt her. I don't believe in it. We need that veneer of civility."

Harry looked back at Carole, who was going through the bottom of my bowl for the smaller of the popped kernels.

Had I been Harry, I would have wished them both the best and moved on. But he was captivated. She'd lied to him, but he didn't care. He told me later it was the Carpool Companions idea that put him over the top. By taking what he'd done to her and spinning it around like that, she'd justified his intuitive feeling about her. She'd proven she was special.

And for Harry, somehow, she had charisma. Great film stars have a quality that makes you watch them, no matter what they're doing. Harry had to watch Carole eating that popcorn. Reuben didn't seem that smitten by her, but Harry did.

On the other hand, he had to acknowledge Reuben. He was her roommate. He was standing right there.

"Well . . . all right, then. You should both stay with me," Harry said finally. "Until you get your business established. You can't start up a company from an unoccupied ledge in a boulder. If the idea of charity bothers you, we'll keep track; we'll have a nominal rent and you can pay me back when you're taking money in."

Reuben looked at him suspiciously. "Guess not," he said.

"Hey," said Harry. "Let me be hospitable. I misunderstood before. I thought you were a bad guy."

"Now you just think I'm an idiot," said Reuben. "I know what you're trying to do."

"I'm trying to do something decent. If you don't like it you don't have to stay."

Reuben looked at Carole, who looked thoughtfully at her sneakered feet, which were up on the corner of my kitchen table.

"The cave will always be there," said Harry.

Reuben shook his head. "Somebody else'll take it."

"Who?" snorted Harry. "Pogo?"

"It is gonna get colder," Carole ruminated. "And everybody around here freaks if you light a fire." She looked at Harry doubtfully. "I don't know, though. I walk a lot now. It's exercise. I'm afraid if I live in a house I'm gonna get cellulite."

They entered into negotiations. Reuben didn't trust Harry, and Carole didn't seem wild about him either, but that item about winter coming on carried weight. It gets chilly in Laguna in wintertime. They finally agreed to stay in the castle for a night and see how it went. Harry was delighted.

"I sense that this is a historic occasion," he said.

I walked the three of them to my door. As they went out, Carole looked me up and down critically and said, "You should have some green vegetables."

"Why?" I asked. "Do I look sick or something?"

"No, I mean for guests."

. . .

The inland wing of Harry's home, into which Carole and Reuben moved, was pretty beat up; it had lumber in it, and a lot of sawdust and regular dust. Dirt too, and other debris. But there were lots of rooms, and a huge bathroom with a big circular tub in it. There was no ocean view, but you could look out over Aliso Viejo to the east. And if you walked around to the front of the building you could see the ocean. After a rain you could see Catalina. Carole and Reuben stayed there that night, and the next morning, Harry made another suggestion.

He told Carole he didn't want her riding the freeway with strangers, and offered to hire her exclusively. He said he'd pay two hundred dollars a day, a hundred up and a hundred back, if she'd ride only with him. She didn't like the "exclusive" part. Harry ended up driving to work that day with Reuben, who only got $30.

I got in at 9:30 that morning and dropped my Hot 99 list on Harry's desk; he was in the weight room. I was in my office around 10 A.M. when I got a one-page fax from him. He occasionally faxed me from his end of the building. At the top of the page were five words: Beatles, Jesus, Elvis, Marilyn, Einstein.

Below the names was written, "Get this guy away from me."

Harry's office was the biggest in our plant, naturally, and had windows on two walls, facing the Wilshire-Janssen intersection. It featured a big desk, a glass-topped table, two long couches at right angles under the windows and Harry's favorite article of furniture: a $4,000 full-length vibrating recliner with four-way massage capability. He liked to read magazines in it after his workouts. There were framed covers on the walls, including our first one, featuring Daniel J. Travanti. On the desk was the only actual book in the room: *Great Thoughts,* compiled by George Seldes. When I came in, Harry was seated at the desk, slashing distractedly at my list with a pen while Reuben sat on one of the couches, droning.

". . . gave up on that, but then I thought you could do an *X-Files* kind of thing as a movie only like *I Spy,* with one black and one white, but then they did *Men in Black.*"

"Quite a top five," I said as I entered.

Harry looked up eagerly. "See? God, sex, rock, movies and brains. It hasn't got sports but you can put Babe Ruth and Ali next and then you've got everything, magnificent seven: black, white, man, woman, birth, death, infinity. I spackled in a few other important people farther down, so I had to bump a few of yours. Also, Number Ninety-nine should be somebody odd, like Superman. No—we'll argue later. I want you to give Reuben the tour. Please."

This was a rarity—Harry begging.

Reuben followed me down the hall, past the conference room, the sales offices and the small studio we used for in-house photo shoots. The *Who's Hot* office layout was simple—one hallway, stretching the length of the second floor, with sales on the left, editorial on the right and the reception area in the middle. If you walked in the main door you'd be facing Bobbi LaMott's big reception counter across a tile entryway featuring more old covers on the walls, going back to Shelley Long. Harry's office was at the extreme left end of the hall, past sales. My office was all the way down to the right.

"You got some babes in here," said Reuben, peering into the offices as we walked.

"Harry believes in fitness," I said. "Especially in sales, he thinks it's good to make an impressive appearance. About half of the women here have SAG cards."

"I suppose you're used to it," he said.

"You never get used to it."

Reuben stopped to stare at the framed covers in reception. Then he leaned over Bobbi LaMott's desk, smiled beatifically and hideously at her and said, "I'm the new vice president in charge of interpersonal relationships."

Bobbi punched a phone button. "*Who's Hot/Who's Not . . .*"

"She does that all day," I said. "She won't be able to talk to you, Reuben."

He watched as she rose to take a fax out of her machine. Then he joined me over by the covers on the walls flanking the entrance door.

"What would you say my chances are?" he asked me.

"Million to one," I said promptly. "No. Billion."

"Why'd you revise it?" he asked. "Notice my mole?"

"The only reason you even get a number is you're tall, and Bobbi says she'll never go out with anyone who isn't taller than she is."

"So there is a chance."

"No. No. There is no chance. I said a billion to one. What would your chances be if you personally went to war with China?"

After all, Reuben was discussing the most attractive woman in the building, which meant one of the most attractive women in the hemisphere. Bobbi was about five-nine, sleek and slim, with thick blonde hair and big blues and long legs. She complemented her stunning looks by dressing impeccably. Reuben, on the other hand, had been sleeping for some time in what amounted to a shallow grave. You expected bugs to crawl out of his pockets. His hair had that greasy, stringy look that was never really in. He was all un-identified stains.

"Aren't you with Carole, anyway?" I asked.

He snorted. "Like there's a comparison."

It seemed to me he should have been a little more loyal, but before I got too righteous I had to recall that when Bobbi LaMott first came to work with us, Joanne had whapped me once for star-ing. I still stared sometimes, but casually, without hope. Bobbi and I were the same height. Her rule was a silly one, I thought. But it clearly disqualified me. Women who are five-nine are always taller than men who are five-nine.

I assumed Bobbi would eventually pair up with a man who looked like a male version of herself. Maybe somebody in the film industry. Bobbi loved movies; even old ones. Everything that hap-pened reminded her of a movie. She had a title for almost every situation.

"What's wrong with me?" demanded Reuben. "Is it my clothes? I don't look like money?"

"Well, you're a little oily," I allowed. "For better or worse, Reuben, people put a value on personal appearance."

"That's such bullshit," said Reuben, shooting a glare at Bobbi.

"And yet dese are da conditions dat prevail," I said.

That got Reuben scratching his head—or anyway, something got Reuben scratching his head—and we moved on toward my office. But there wasn't much to see on the editorial side of the hall, so our tour bogged down. Harry had all the interesting rooms and most of the prettiest people on his side of the building. On the editorial side, all we had was the coffee alcove.

Reuben drifted back to Bobbi's area. I was trying to decide what else to do with him when the entrance door opened and Art Klee, star of the recent film *Smoker's Cough,* came through . . . armed. He wore a long, charcoal-colored light overcoat and carried a weapon like an old tommy gun, with a little hopper attached to it. He turned to the left, past Bobbi's desk, and strode down the hall toward Harry's office. The gun was partially concealed under his coat, but the barrel stuck out below, pointed at the carpet. I saw salespeople dive out of his way.

In his wake, Bobbi LaMott leaned over her counter, staring after him.

"I thought he was gonna shoot me," she said weakly. "I thought it was *Three Days of the Condor*." Her head swiveled toward me. "Is he gonna shoot Harry?"

"Well," I said, moving forward toward Harry's office, "maybe not. He's an actor."

SIX

Actors are not notably violent. Many film actors have to act tough from time to time, and handle weapons, but you rarely hear of an actor killing anyone. And that's remarkable, because actors lead frustrating lives. They're always on display, and easy to dismiss. They spend most of their lives not getting the part.

Art Klee had done better than 99 percent. He had started out on *Manhattan Live,* the sketch comedy show, and then moved on to Hollywood. A couple of his early movies were big hits. In recent years he hadn't been so successful, but everyone still knew who he was, and he still did a movie now and then. They just weren't eagerly anticipated.

Art wasn't poor. He wasn't out of work. But he wasn't hot either, and consequently, he often appeared in our Not section. In fact, Harry, who knew him, had made a kind of running gag out of it, especially in the last issue, when Klee had broken the consecutive appearances record previously held by Eddie Friend.

One man's joke, however, can be another's unforgivable insult, and judging by Klee's demeanor as he'd entered the office, he was irate enough to go beyond typical actor behavior. As I hurried down the corridor I heard shouting from beyond the half-open door of Harry's office. Ernie Scheffing darted out of *his* office and past me, toward reception, his eyes fixed straight ahead. Emily Hahn, Harry's secretary, whose station was just outside Harry's door, wasn't visible. I hoped she was in the rest room, on a break, or under her desk. If she was in Harry's office she could be in for an ordeal.

"What's up?" asked Reuben from behind me. I raised a hand to indicate caution.

As I neared Harry's door, I saw Emily Hahn's feet, under her desk. So she was okay. I then glanced into the conference room and saw Joanne's legs; she was crouched under the big table. She'd apparently gotten herself stranded. I detoured into the conference room and went under the table to join her for a moment.

On my knees, I murmured, "You're visible from the hall."

She scrambled back awkwardly, farther under. Joanne looked good no matter what she was doing. In the early days of our relationship, we had had a powerful encounter on the floor of her apartment, and now, inappropriately, it came back to me.

We saw a couple more salesmen hustle down the hallway, right to left, toward reception and away from Harry's office. It was a rare opportunity for me to look braver than every other male employee in the building. Apparently I was the only one who had noticed that Art Klee's weapon was a paintball gun.

I'd never gone paintballing, but Harry liked it. Once a month or so he'd journey out to one of these layouts they have around L.A. where you can play war. They've got model Vietnams and Beiruts and Bosnias set up on the paintball grounds; teenagers and grown men can sneak up on each other and fire away.

Harry never forced the staff to go paintballing. He encouraged us to do it, to hone our competitive edge, but he didn't insist. One time at a company picnic at the castle he set up some soda cans in his backyard and some of us took a turn. I splattered two cans on my third hipshot—knocked one into another—and quit. I knew I couldn't top that. The bullets were small, bright orange balls; they

64

were like high-velocity gumballs. The weapon was a pump gun, with a hopper attached. If I'd had such a gun as a kid, Bloomington, Illinois, would be all one color today.

I knew it was wrong to let Joanne cower in mortal fear like that. Art Klee was unlikely to kill anyone with such a weapon. On the other hand, the gun WAS dangerous. At the paintball field the combatants had to wear a goalie-type mask and protective suit. Those balls came out of the barrel mighty fast. In Carole Spangler's phrase, they could put your eye out. At the very least they would raise welts, especially at close range. I leaned forward and whispered in Joanne's ear.

"You'll be all right here."

I started to crawl away. She clutched my thigh—something I would have bet she'd never do again.

"Where are you going?" she whispered anxiously.

"I'm gonna ask for more money. Now's the time, when he's distracted."

"Are you crazy? That guy's got a gun!"

"That makes it tricky," I admitted.

Her eyes widened as I moved out from under the table. She had *never* looked at me like that before. Even when I hit my head on the bottom edge, I didn't completely spoil the effect.

Of course, then I had to go on into Harry's office.

Reuben had waited for me in the corridor; I was still his guide. I held up a hand again and edged to Harry's half-open door. I couldn't see either Klee or Harry, but they were audible, vilifying each other. As I passed Emily Hahn's desk, I leaned over and looked under it. Harry had told her to submarine whenever she saw a threatening situation developing. Emily was around sixty, with frosted hair; the only older woman on Harry's side of the building. He deferred to her on all matters involving correspondence. She treated him as if he were the most troublesome of her sons.

She sat decorously on the floor, with her legs tucked to the side and her skirt over her knees. Her eyes were big behind her glasses as she looked up at me; she shook her head slowly.

"It's okay," I told her softly. "All he's got—"

There was a crashing sound and a roar of rage and pain from the office; then some more crashing and some more roaring. Emily flinched at the first roar, which was from Harry. I did too. Then I straightened up, tiptoed forward and took a quick glimpse through the doorway.

I ducked my head back out again. Inside, Harry and Art Klee had each taken cover. Klee had tipped over Harry's glass-topped table and gotten behind it, over in the near right corner. There was an orange splotch on the glass and another on the wall behind Klee, which indicated that Harry had somehow gotten hold of his own paintball gun. I hadn't seen Harry on my look in, but I heard him bellowing from behind his desk, which was spattered as well. Between Harry and Klee, in no-man's-land, the beautiful black recliner had taken at least two hits. Harry and Klee were screaming names at each other, apparently popping up to fire and then crouching back down.

"Can't take it, can ya!" and "Come and get me, has-been!" came from behind Harry's desk. I heard a "How do you like it" and a few random "assholes" from Klee. It was loud and banal.

The normal Joe Hoyle would have said, "Well; they want to be alone," and gone back to editorial. But since my breakup with Joanne I hadn't been myself; I'd been less concerned about getting hurt. I took a big breath to compose myself, trotted in place and wiggled my wrists to loosen up and then sneaked into the office, following the contour of the right-hand wall. As a child playing similar games, I'd learned to move silently. Klee was hunkered down with his back to me, popping up to shoot off his left shoulder at Harry. When I got near enough, I reached over his head and latched onto the paintball gun by the barrel. Klee immediately jerked it away, pulling me partially over his right shoulder, but

Reuben came up on his left and the three of us wrestled for the gun while Harry peeked out from cover.

"Got it?" called Harry.

"Leggo," snarled Klee, his teeth gritted. He was stocky and strong. We all twisted the barrel strenuously, back and forth. Klee kicked my shin and I momentarily lost my grip. Reuben suddenly relaxed *his* grip and Klee, yanking without resistance, cracked his knuckles on the edge of the table. Reuben then wrenched the gun free and spun away.

Harry emerged from behind his desk. He had an orange sunburst on his left shirtsleeve and another on his right shoulder. His glasses were awry, and he carried his gun in his right hand.

"Yo," he said, breathing heavily. "Thanks for the backup."

Reuben stood in front of Harry's desk and pensively pumped the barrel of Klee's gun back.

"Hey," said Harry.

Reuben fired from the hip; Harry hit the floor. Klee and I went down too. The back of Harry's chair took a direct hit; his pen set was blasted off his desk.

It wasn't really Reuben's fault; you couldn't hold one of those paintball guns without shooting it at least once. Reuben limited himself to just the one shot. Then he lowered the barrel and looked down at all of us.

"Fun," he said. He dropped the weapon on the desk, next to Harry's.

Harry rose, coming up with the pen, minus the holder. He wasn't mad. "Bring you along next time I go," he said.

Harry sat on the edge of his desk. He faced Art Klee, who had righted an overturned chair and was resting in it, panting and glowering. Klee's face was blotchy. He'd taken a hit on his hip, high up on his pants leg. He was sweaty, and seemed uncomfortable. Of course, they were both in pain, but neither would rub.

"Shame," said Harry.

"You've had me in that Not section seventy-four weeks in a

row," Klee replied bitterly between breaths. "That's a year and a half."

"Almost," Harry agreed.

"What about *Smoker's Cough*? That's an A picture. I carried it. You've got this punk Sterling Fleger on the Hot list off the cabdriver part in that picture, and not me. I was the lead, he had a bit! I gave him the part."

"*He* made me laugh," said Harry.

"Like you know what's funny."

"I have an excellent sense of humor," said Harry. "I'm not funny myself, but I can recognize it."

"I *gave* that guy the laughs. To make the scene work."

"You've been mighty generous the last ten years."

Klee was silent for a moment, then made a dive for the guns on the desk, but Reuben grabbed one and Harry the other before he could reach them. Reuben stood back and pumped the barrel once.

"Who IS this guy?" asked Klee indignantly, staring at Reuben.

"He's my deputy," said Harry, and sat back on the edge of his desk, his gun butt poised on his thigh.

"Look," said Klee. "You gotta stop doing this. I don't know why anybody would read your rag, but some people do. You're hurting me with people. I want you to make it right."

Harry gestured at his spattered walls. "This is supposed to win me over?"

"I told you last week, if I was in the Not section again you'd see me in here. You brought this on yourself. You knew it was gonna happen—you had your goddamn gun right there in the corner."

Harry smirked a bit at that, but he turned stony when Klee continued:

"What the hell is your problem? What did I do to you?"

"Hey," said Harry. "I'm kind to you. It's worse than I say. You've been coasting for years. Getting by on work you did in the *seventies.* How many people get to do that? You're taking up space that could be better filled by a hundred starving actors. Honest to God, Art, every time I see you up on the screen, this . . . wave of indifference comes over me. And I believe that this is not a feeling unique to me, but one I share with many. So when I refer to you as 'not hot,' that's like a kiss, you know? I'm pinching your cheek when you deserve a kick in the ass. I've got a list coming up of the Top Nine Future Nots of the twenty-first century, and you're looking good for it. I'm not going to cut you slack because we were on the same paintball team in Bosnialand. And by the way, the stains better come off that chair"—he pointed at his full-body recliner—"or you owe me a replacement with four different massage capabilities."

Klee sat motionless through this hosing. Then he sighed. Then he stood up.

"Want my gun," he said.

Harry shook his head.

"I'll bring it to the field next time." Harry exhaled, milder now, and ran his hand through his hair, checking for splotches. "You can still do good work, Art. But you have to get the fire goin'."

"Hey," said Art Klee. He was still a good enough actor to convey with one syllable that he'd had enough conversation. He glanced at Reuben, and the gun. Then he walked to the doorway, brushing past me on the way. Once at the door he turned toward Harry.

"You think you can say anything," he said. "Someday I'm gonna sit and watch *your* movie." He looked from Reuben to me, and then back to Harry. "Don't put me on that list," he added. "I won't take any more. I want to be clear: I'm threatening you."

"Is that supposed to be a— Oh," said Harry.

Klee left. Emily Hahn came out from under her desk and into Harry's office to survey the damage. The salespeople and other staff came straggling back down the hall toward us. Harry thanked Reuben for his assistance.

"Took guts to come in here with all that goin' on," he said, shaking Reuben's hand.

Joanne came up to me in the hallway.

"Joe, that was brave, what you did." She seemed shocked.

"Oh, I don't know. You think so?"

Unfortunately, Ted Fairbanks appeared at this point, to take Joanne out to lunch . . . coming down the hall, with his tan and his teeth and his height. He came up to us and said, "Hey, babe," to Joanne, and "What's goin' on?" He put his arm around her.

I went to the men's room. After a moment, Harry took the urinal to my right.

"Bulletin: Paintballs really hurt," he said.

"You really scalded Klee with those remarks you made," I told him. "Might want to lay off him for a while."

"Annhhhh, he needed to be goosed." Harry wasn't worried about Art Klee. He had told me many times that he'd never die at the hands of an actor.

Steve Kluszewski and Jimmy Nations came in as Harry zipped up and turned to look at his paintball splotches in the mirror.

"I'm gonna wear these all day," Harry announced. He started out but Kluszewski stopped him.

"Harry," he said, "a month ago in here you shook my hand, told me I did a good job rebooting the system. Now I'm gonna shake yours." He stuck his hand out and Harry took it. Steve pulled him into an embrace. "Don't let the bastards intimidate you," he said.

"Okay, Steve."

"Did you really shoot Art Klee?" asked Jimmy Nations.

"Wouldn't you?" asked Harry.

"Goddamn," said Jimmy, grinning. "Shit." He walked all around Harry to see where he'd been hit.

I was back in my office when Emily Hahn came in with her notepad. She looked anxious and conspiratorial.

"Now he's getting code," she told me. She held the pad in front of my face.

The top sheet read, ";pd smhr;rd mpb yrm."

It seems idiotic to say the message looked familiar to me, but it did. Undecipherable, but familiar.

"That's not code, it's just garble," I said.

She shook her head. "He had an E-mail on the screen when I went in. From Wesley Willis. And this was it."

The name made me look again. Wesley Willis was a high-level gofer for John Easter, the British tabloid baron. When Easter bought U.S. publications, Willis, an ex-newspaperman from Philadelphia, would go in and turn the place inside out. He was presently running an Easter acquisition called *Rushes*, an L.A. slick similar to ours but not nearly as good.

I looked again. ";pd smhr;rd mpb yrm," it said.

"Millionaire talk," I said finally.

"Some of us take this seriously," she reproved me.

I shrugged.

"I can't read it. I can tell you this: It's Harry's mail."

"You don't think it's our business if he's talking to John Easter?"

"Not yet. Throw it out."

Emily's lips pursed stubbornly.

"I'm in charge of correspondence," she said. "He's bypassing me. There's only one reason he'd be doing that."

"Ask him, then."

"Like he'd tell me." She tore the top page off and slapped it down on my desk. "I'm throwing it away, from me to you. And if you figure it out, and you don't tell, you're a stinker."

·   ·   ·

It's said that rumors are always distorted, but it's been my experience that major office rumors are usually right. The prevailing rumor after Art Klee's visit was that Harry was going to sell *Who's Hot/Who's Not*. The E-mail message kicked it off. It didn't matter that nobody knew what it said. What mattered was who sent it.

Harry'd had offers for the magazine once or twice before, and he'd ignored them. But that was before he bought the castle and agreed to a divorce settlement with Yasmine which was apparently a kind of arterial wound, so it was possible that he needed money.

He seemed, in my judgment, to be on the verge of some grand plunge. At first I'd assumed it was solely personal. I thought he was just dizzy about Carole Spangler. His talk on the porch about on-ramp to on-ramp had been as outlandish, if not as crude, as the way he'd talked after he met Yasmine. The story was still told in the office about the night he introduced Yasmine to a tableful of staff at a magazine awards dinner. He said they'd met on Friday and spent the weekend reinventing sex, right up to their arrival moments before at valet parking. "My tip is bruised," he'd announced. "Right, hon?"

I had thought Harry was focused solely on Carole. It wasn't until Emily showed me that E-mail message that I thought he might have plans for us as well. That was when I remembered the rest of his talk that night—the stuff about doing something of value.

Scary talk, to be sure. If the magazine was sold, Harry's staff could end up not only unemployed, but looking for a new line of work. There weren't a lot of jobs available in our field. You couldn't very well say to yourself, Well, if I lose this job I'll get one just like it in Houston.

Most of us had gone into the entertainment industry because we had loved the movies and TV as kids. And even now, all grown up and well aware that much of the "product" and many of the producers were untalented or ghastly people, we still felt privileged to be on the scene when something fine got done. For better or worse, the people we wrote about had the biggest audience in the history of the world. So our subject was both trivial and enormously influential. We were part of something big. And like the guy who cleaned out the circus tent, we didn't want to leave show business.

"Suppose he sells us to Easter, or Rupert Murdoch?" Neil Purkey demanded one day while a few of us were having lunch at the Bum's Rush. "They've already got their own people. They'd get rid of us."

"Not necessarily," I said. "We've been successful. They might keep things the way they are. We're so small, I don't think Murdoch would change us."

"Easter would," said Neil.

"Harry wouldn't sell," said Bobbi LaMott. "Would he?"

I didn't know why Bobbi would even care. She was young, she'd only been with us two years, and she was so gorgeous that she was unlikely to stay unemployed five minutes longer than she wanted to. But some of the rest of us were in a different spot. We'd stayed too long. Harry had raised our salaries until we were practically unemployable elsewhere.

The rumor crescendoed, along with the staff's anxiety, for a week following Art Klee's visit in mid-October. Finally, on a Friday afternoon, a bunch of us went into Harry's office and asked him point-blank if he intended to sell the shop.

The delegation included Neil Purkey, Joanne and me, from editorial; Eden Ramos and Ernie Scheffing, from sales; Peter Hood, from the art department; Steve Kluszewski and Jimmy Nations, from production; and Kay Jardine from word processing. Everybody was either a department head or a longtime employee except for Jimmy Nations, who just really wanted to be there.

Harry leaned back in his chair while we ranged ourselves around the room. He offered us all the chance to sit in the recliner, but nobody did.

Eden started things off for us because she was generally considered the most professional and even-tempered of the department heads.

"We won't keep you, Harry," she said. "We're here to ask two questions, really. Are you selling the plant, and if so, to whom?"

"And what happens to us and when," added Joanne. "That's four."

Harry looked from Joanne to his window.

"Let me tell you a story," he said, and we knew we were in trouble.

"When I started this place, I said, 'By the time I'm forty-five, I'm gonna have the top entertainment magazine in the world.' Well, we came in ahead of schedule. And ever since, I've been going along, like you, day to day. Circulation flattened out, and I let it. I had some vague ideas about doing something more someday, but nothing specific. I was coasting, like Art Klee.

"And then one night, recently, I encountered someone who woke me up. Someone . . . special, who woke me to a larger purpose I'd almost forgotten. See, we all have within us some great effort. If we don't make that effort—if we settle—then we're cheating ourselves and we're going to die with the sudden realization that we wasted our time here. Which, I believe, is followed by an eternity of nothingness."

There was a brief pause.

"So who's the buyer?" Joanne asked.

Harry gazed at her evenly.

"I've gotten some interesting offers lately."

There was movement among us. Neil Purkey murmured, "When Harry Poe gets a midlife crisis, everybody gets a midlife crisis."

"I'm sorry, Neil, say again?" asked Harry.

"What's the point of knocking ourselves out if you're going to sell us to John Easter or somebody else who's going to fire all of us?" demanded Neil.

Harry took a deep breath. "I'm not saying I'm selling. I'm not saying I'm not. If you can't stand the uncertainty, I'll expand the severance agreement to include quitting: Anyone who wants to leave can have two weeks' pay for every six months they've worked here."

I cast a glance around at my colleagues. I wouldn't say it was a family feeling we all had, but it was close. We'd seen each other angry and silly; we knew how we all reacted under pressure at work. We had a common past.

"Not exactly a golden parachute," remarked Joanne.

Harry's eyes narrowed a bit.

"I don't owe you one," he said.

"*You'll* get one," said Neil.

Harry chuckled. He was getting mad. "Neil, you want to write. You're what, thirty-eight? It's now or never." He looked to the rest of us. "This place is mine. I guess what I do is up to me."

"Over the years, we've been a team," I said. Harry transferred his gaze to me.

"Teams get sold," he observed.

"We've been friends too," I said.

Harry took on a look of puzzled exasperation.

"I'm not selling you to the Comancheros," he said. "You all seem to think I owe you something. I'm not behind with the checks. You get benefits and bonuses. You're free to leave me anytime; I should be free to leave you."

"You've got no right to sell us without at least giving us a chance for an employee buyout," said Ernie Scheffing.

Harry laughed. I sighed. Ernie's remark, I knew, had closed out the meeting. Harry spoke affably.

" 'No right.' Wow. Well, first off, Ern, you can't compete with the offers I'm getting. And second off, no *right*? Gee, we disagree there. 'Cause if you'll excuse my saying so, this is my motherfucking-

bat and ball, and I've got a 'right' to sell it or give it away or blow it out my ass. And if you think I don't, try and stop me." He looked brightly around at the rest of us.

That seemed to cover everything, so we left.

SEVEN

At home that night I drafted a resume. I hadn't compiled one for years, and I felt I should have a document handy, with boldface stress on my accomplishments. I think several of us at *Who's Hot* were doing much the same thing that night.

I was prepared to use positive distortion, but I knew not to lie outright. I'd seen people escorted from the building because it turned out they didn't have the degree they said they had. I myself had had a bad experience once with lying outright.

EDUCATION: Attended Peppard College, Eugene, Ill.

I had to put "attended"; I left before graduating. It was suggested that I go. I got thrown out for claiming to have cowritten a play with Mark Twain.

As a sophomore, I wanted to impress a girl in the theater department, so I enrolled in a playwrighting class and worked up a one-act for a competition; the three best were to be shown in the student theater. Mine was a kind of fantasy Western, but it wasn't really very good. It had Norse gods and gunfighters in it, but it seemed to need even more. So I gave it a coauthor. I wrote a little preface for the program stating that the play was an elaboration of notes Mark Twain left with my great-grandmother Anna when he was on his last visit to Hannibal, Missouri, in 1902.

The truth was that Twain did go back to Hannibal in 1902, but as far as I know he didn't spend any time with Anna. He wrote several plays and fragments of plays in his life, though, most of which went unproduced. And Anna did live in Hannibal at the time. So what I was saying wasn't impossible. It was just false.

At the time, I preferred to think of it as a witty hoax. I got the idea from the story of William Ireland, who as a teenager in England in the 1790s claimed to have found a lost Shakespeare play called *Vortigern and Rowena*. For a while, people believed the play was genuine. It even opened in London before everyone realized the kid wrote the thing himself.

My one-act was one of the three that got staged. It was awful. But it got some local press, and somehow word got out on the AP wire that a lost Mark Twain play had been performed by college students in southern Illinois.

It was a revelation to me, how much interest some people took in Mark Twain and his itinerary. Three days after we opened a reporter called me to ask when precisely Samuel Clemens saw my great-grandmother, and where, and asking where were the notes. The next thing I knew I was being asked by the head of the theater and English departments to produce the original fragments. I said it was more like an oral family tradition.

My deception collapsed when another reporter called up my mother in Bloomington and she said, "Oh, he's teasing you."

Maybe a tougher kid could have stuck it out. Had it happened a few years later, when deconstruction was popular, I might have claimed the play was a refutation of the concept of individual authorship or something. Back then, though, I was a fraud. Once my mom tore off my whiskers I was demoralized.

Mom called and said she was very disappointed.

I wrote out a statement and read it to the reporters who'd

come to campus, and they went away. Nobody preferred charges. For a while there was talk of a lawsuit by Samuel Clemens' descendants, but all that happened was that every newspaper in the area used the "not according to Hoyle" line about me. The girl I'd meant to impress . . . well, it goes without saying.

I had to meet with Dean Pillette, a very grim and solid man. He did a lot of fund-raising for Peppard, and told me that his job was about to become more difficult, because it would be hard to sell people on a school that produced flimflam artists such as myself. He further informed me that I would do better elsewhere, or if I didn't, so what.

Harry Poe lived down the hall in my dorm. As I was packing to leave he came into my room and said, "This is unfair. You didn't plagiarize. It was the *opposite* of plagiarism. You were giving Twain extra *credit*."

I returned to Bloomington. For a while I was mad at everybody for catching me. I agreed with Harry. I thought the Peppard faculty and administrators had overreacted. But my dad, never a chatterbox, had a single comment on what I'd done:

"There's already enough bullshit in the world."

The long-term effect of the incident was that I eventually became meticulous about my work. Condensed for my resume, the story became "Attended Peppard College."

MARITAL STATUS: I doodled here, writing, "Should have married Joanne." Then I crossed it out. No prospective employer wants to read expressions of regret in a resume. I wasn't even sure I meant what I wrote. Marriage was a mystery to me.

I was married for eighteen months in my twenties, in Chicago, to a barmaid as dizzy as I was. We weren't ready. We didn't have kids, which was a mercy. Since then, I'd been more careful.

PREVIOUS EMPLOYMENT: My first job after college was as a temporary office worker. My company sent me here and there around Chicago for a day or a week. I worked at the Museum of Science and Industry, operating a stamping machine. I worked at an old folks' home on the South Side, typing up the script for their annual variety show. That was because I'd had experience as a playwright.

Later I got a job as a telex operator at a newspaper in the Loop, but telex was a dying language. All the telexes got replaced by computers with phone modems. By the time Harry came through town a few years later, on his way out west, I was inputting technical manuals and living primarily on turkey wings and hash browns. Harry took me out for a drink at Riccardo's and said he had an idea for a magazine.

"Everybody loves showbiz," he said. "Somebody's always hot and somebody's always not." He had the title even then.

Harry had start-up money behind him—his father's—but it was limited. "Dad says he won't support me a day past thirty." Somehow Harry had convinced his dad that he could make a success of an entertainment slick, with no previous experience besides running the college paper and spending three years as a grunt at *This Week in Business*.

Harry said he could use me: "You knew more trivia than anybody else in the dorm."

This was true. When I was a kid in Bloomington, there wasn't much excitement. Everyone just flew over us. Movies were my great energy source. Once when I had the flu, I watched Burt Lancaster in *The Rainmaker* on TV, and I absorbed so much vitality from him that I was cured; when the movie ended I went out in the side yard and climbed a tree.

I read the entire cast list too; not just the star names. By the time I got to college I knew Jack Elam from Barbara Luna. But so did other people. I didn't know why Harry wanted me specifically.

"Because of what happened at school," he said confidently, signaling our waiter. "You won't let us get in trouble."

PRESENT EMPLOYER: For years I did the final read on every issue. "Trivia yes, bullshit no" was my motto. I was good on typos;

the only bad one I ever missed was when we called Bruce Willis the fecal point of studio strategy one year. I especially liked Where Did They Go? I enjoyed meeting some of the old actors from when I was growing up. Harry used to get sore when I'd write occasionally about people who'd never been hot. "Who the hell is Dub Taylor?" he'd demand. "Who is Dabbs Greer? Who are these Dubs and Dabbs?" But I liked to sneak in little bits about those old guys now and then. They were the infantry of Hollywood. They'd been everywhere. And on TV back in Bloomington, they'd been like relatives to me.

All those years at *Who's Hot* made me look steady on the resume, but they also made me look inert. I listed my responsibilities, stretching them out as much as possible, but I still ended up short. If your entire positive list of accomplishments comes in under a page, it looks bad. Triple spacing doesn't fool anybody.

·   ·   ·

I shelved the resume. On my desk I had notes for an old, unpublished list—my Should've Been Hot list. A pointless exercise. As Joanne had once remarked, the magazine wasn't called *Who Should Be Hot*. I'd always felt, though, that there were many performers who had never got the credit they deserved, like Billy Gray, Zohra Lampert, and the Amazing Rhythm Aces. I'd never completed the list, though; there was no place for these people at *Who's Hot*.

I didn't feel so hot myself. Joanne had intimated that I wasn't going anywhere, but I hadn't fully realized it until I tried to type my resume up.

I walked from living room to kitchen and back. Sashi looked up hopefully as I passed the pantry. I wondered if Harry would take me along on his next project. I wondered how long I'd last if he didn't. For nearly my entire life, I'd been supported by either my father or Harry Poe.

This thought led me to a perverse and self-destructive decision.

I'm sure it was because of the breakup with Joanne. Everything I did around this time was uncharacteristic.

Sometimes you get a delayed effect after a breakup. It hurts more—and longer—than you think it's going to. You enter a period of despair characterized by a lack of concern about what happens to you. Things that would ordinarily scare you don't. Caution seems pointless. After all, caution got you here.

Joanne hadn't used the word "wienie" when she moved out, but it had been hovering, unspoken, as a subtext to her other remarks. The implication was that I had become one of those company men who work at the same desk until they become invisible. Afraid to take a chance. And maybe she was right. Looked at from her point of view, I was a blank slate. And so she'd left me.

It struck me, suddenly, as a ridiculous way for a man to live. I hadn't gambled, but I'd lost. And here I was, worrying about losing my job. Worrying about having my stagnant life disrupted. Was it for this that the Hoyles had emigrated from England at some point in the 1800s, we weren't quite sure when? So that the line could culminate in a wienie?

I grabbed a jacket, walked to the front door and looked at my image in the hall mirror.

"Character, here we come," I told it.

·   ·   ·

Harry's kitchen was in the center section of his vast downstairs, surrounded by open areas with long tables and conversation pits. The kitchen was an elevated island with another island inside it, consisting of a counter and a four-burner range. Since the building was so big and hard to heat, on a cool night everyone tended to gravitate toward the kitchen.

On this evening Harry's guests included Carole Spangler, Reuben Schifrin, and four other people from the streets of Laguna. They were sitting at one of the long tables just off the kitchen, eating some noodle dish. Harry introduced me to the strangers—their names were Paul, Donna, Stevie and Lorenzo.

Reuben had new clothes. Harry had gotten him shirts, two pair of pants, shoes, socks, underwear and a London Fog coat after his heroism in the battle with Art Klee. Carole wore a new sweater—a big, bulky green one. The other guests were pretty much in tatters, but they seemed in good spirits, digging in. They had beer, but I noticed Carole wasn't drinking.

Harry was bright-eyed. When he met me at the door he murmured, "Good news tonight: She and Reuben want separate rooms."

He got louder and more expansive as we reached the guests, announcing, "This is the core group of the new movement." He gestured at the table. "These are the shock troops. Everyone here is motivated. Ready to start over."

"I'm TIRED of peeing on the mattress!" announced Carole Spangler, pounding her fork-holding fist on the table.

"I'm tired of sleeping out fuckin' side," muttered Stevie, the youngest-looking of the men.

Harry gestured for me to sit down. "It's gonna be another magazine. *Second Chances*. I got the idea from Carole. Up from the gutter and back from the dead. It's gonna feature people who came back from total failure. Inspirational. The hook is, the magazine is gonna be staffed entirely by homeless people."

"Entirely," I repeated.

"And that's just the start. There's a big old Not section out there"—he gestured toward the outdoors. "I'm gonna help people cross over. It's gonna be a company too. My company. Second Chances Inc. Staffed by the homeless."

"The company'll be all homeless too?"

"Everybody. We'll eventually spin it off into studios and factories. There's no limit to what we can do, because we have the core resources everywhere."

"A homeless chief financial officer?"

Harry shrugged. "We might have to adjust the tuning. But yeah. Sure. You know, I never thought about the homeless as a source of energy until Carole here. I was oblivious."

"Do they have to stay homeless? Is that a rule?"

"No, you dink. They just start out that way. And whoever else we hire has to start out that way. You'll be the exception, because you're always the exception. You're in on the grandfather clause."

The bearded man named Lorenzo, seated the farthest down the table, raised his hand, like a student.

"I think you'll find, sir," he said to Harry, leaning forward until his hair was in his plate, "that the people down at the beach, you don't have enough, and most of them are unemployable." He sat back, then leaned forward suddenly and added, "Assholes."

Harry nodded politely. "I don't expect to use everybody. But everybody we *use* will be homeless. Except Joe, of course. Joe goes where I go."

"About that," I said, and stopped. Harry looked at me, mildly curious.

"Yeah?" he asked.

I took a deep breath and went ahead.

"I quit."

Harry nodded, chewing, and put down his fork. He picked up a paper towel and wiped his mouth.

"Uh-huh. Uh-huh." He kept nodding.

"He don't like the idea," said Reuben.

"He doesn't like us," said Carole Spangler.

"No-no, no, it's not that," I said. "I decided this at home, tonight. That's why I came over. I'm just leaving. I'm out. I think it's best. Time for a change. New vistas." I coughed.

Harry looked at me speculatively.

"What, did you see a movie?"

"No, I just think it's best."

He twisted his last noodles up onto his fork. The gang down

the table were already through eating and were lighting up. It was smoke-'em-if-you-got-'em at Harry's table tonight.

"Going to another magazine?" he asked finally.

"Not that I know of."

"What are you gonna do then? Get a job playing Goofy on the Big Red Boat?"

I kept my composure.

"With that severance deal you offered I'll have a year's pay coming," I told him.

Harry chuckled, as if he suddenly got it.

"This is a gesture," he said. "I must have come on too tough today. You're rebelling. It's all right. You want some linguini? I made it myself. We'll start over. You didn't say it, I didn't hear it, you're still aboard. I know you're gonna want to be in on *Second Chances*." He leaned forward to murmur, "This is what the bonus time was for."

"Well, that's all great and everything. You know. Helping the homeless. That's good of you, Harry. But really, I've decided. You should count me out."

Harry dropped his paper towel on his plate. He sat back and looked all around his dining area.

"You're walking out on me," he said.

"No, it's not about you."

"How can it not be about me? I'm the one you're quitting."

I got irritated.

"I don't care, I'm the one who's leaving. It's about ME, get it? Not you. Me. It's all about m . . ." My voice trailed off as I glanced around at Harry's guests. Many of them had probably, at some point, made a career decision similar to the one I was making now.

"Kind of full of yourself, aren't you?" said Carole Spangler, regarding me through cigarette smoke.

I rubbed my forehead. Harry leaned forward until his head was beside mine, and spoke quietly toward the floor.

"Joe, some people don't make it on their own. Look around the table. Tip of the iceberg."

I was offended. He had me homeless already.

"Well, if I go under, I'll qualify for your new thing here," I told him.

Harry had a kind of lazy left eye that evidenced itself sometimes when he was at the end of his patience. It would half-close on such occasions. It had done this at the end of the meeting in his office that day, and it did so now. He rose from the table.

"Okay," he said. "You got six months' health insurance."

I cleared my throat. "I'll stay to train a replacement."

"No. I want you out by Friday."

He took his plate, left the table and stepped up into the kitchen. I rose, feeling as awkward as I could remember. Harry's new team was looking at me.

I went to the kitchen to say good-bye. Harry was rinsing his plate.

"Estelita quit too," he said. "She doesn't approve of my guests."

"Harry, we've been friends a long time. You shouldn't take this personally."

"Hey," he said. "I'm fine. I've found my true calling. You should be so lucky."

· · ·

My decision to leave *Who's Hot* caused a seismic disturbance at work. People came into my office one by one to stare at me for the rest of the week. Harry stayed down at his end of the hall and spoke to me only when necessary.

Most of my visitors believed I was quitting because I knew John Easter was going to buy the magazine and fire everyone. I denied having this knowledge, but no one seemed to believe me. Neil Purkey said, "I thought we were friends," and walked out on me.

When Joanne came in, the morning the news broke, she was as wide-eyed as she'd been under the table in the conference room. She looked at me as if I were morphing. "Harry says I'm supposed to take over final read," she said. She sounded tentative, which was rare. I nodded and turned to my screen. She pulled up a chair and sat beside me.

I felt pretty strong. I could sense her attention, her hesitance. I'd done something stupid and she'd noticed me again.

"Final read is important," I said. "You can catch a thousand things, but when the thousand and first gets by, you'll be to blame. So when you feel yourself getting bored and bleeping over the words, read out loud. You'll stay more alert. If that gets too boring, use different voices on alternate paragraphs. You have to go fast, though."

"Will we get fired when Harry sells?" she asked.

"I don't know."

"You can't even tell me?"

I leaned back in my chair and looked at her sadly.

"This is Orville Redenbacher all over again. I said I don't know. Have I ever lied to you?"

She looked at me warily. "How would I know?"

"What I'm doing," I said patiently, "has nothing to do with John Easter. It's just me. It has no significance. It's just me."

We were silent for a moment, while I brought the contents page up on screen.

"You're sure acting different," she said.

Harry brought Carole Spangler up north with him twice that week and showed her around the office. She was sober, and seemed a bit testy about it. I saw her come in the first morning. Harry introduced her to Bobbi LaMott and the two women eyed each other curiously. Carole said, "So you're Reuben's wet dream." Bobbi had no immediate comeback. On both days, Carole left work before Harry did, over his protests, to carpool-companion her way back down south.

On Friday afternoon, Neil told me to come to the conference room because Harry wanted to discuss the new alignment in editorial after I left. When I got there, pretty much everybody in the office was present. They had a cake. It said, "Love and Get Out." Harry made a couple remarks to the assembled group.

"Joe was our Cal Ripken, although he usually didn't get here until the second inning."

He said we went a long way back, and how they were all going to miss me. Then he gave me a little package. I opened it and found a ballpoint pen.

"It's a memo pen," he explained. "Records your thoughts. Up to a minute and a half. You talk into it. I got one for myself. Sudden thought, pull it out."

I also got a year's subscription to *TV Guide,* to match my year's worth of severance, and a nice briefcase in case I ever chose to work again.

Two or three people called for a speech, so I said *Who's Hot/ Who's Not* had been my second family, and that I thought we'd done good work over the years. I looked at Joanne, and then around.

"I'll miss you," I said. "And I'll think of you whenever I . . . talk to my pen."

Emily Hahn kissed me. Peter Hood, the art department head, shook my hand and said, "We should all jump before we're pushed, yes?" Joanne gave me a little hug and a "Good luck, Joe," and went down the hall to her office. I'd hoped she'd break down, but she was brave. A few others said good-bye. And like that, it was over.

In the parking structure, as I got into my old Taurus, I heard footsteps—too heavy for Joanne.

Harry leaned down and peered into my eyes, clearly still puzzled.

"Is it because I put the Beatles ahead of Christ?" he asked.

"Harry, it's your magazine and your list. You can put the Archies ahead of Christ. This is just something I gotta do."

As I turned the key in the ignition, Harry's expression changed. He got his Eureka! look and pounded my roof.

"It's Joanne!"

He walked beside the car as I backed out of my space.

"You're doing this because of her. To show her something. Is that it? Because that's really lame, Joe. That's idiotic. She's already gone. It's like you're being henpecked posthumously. You know? You're being whipped by a woman you can't even sleep with."

I shifted out of reverse.

"I sincerely hope you've begun to do better," I said, and left.

EIGHT

The economic panic would hit later, I figured. For now I was just eager to get home and never make the trip again. I felt I'd exhausted my driving luck over the years.

Two blocks shy of the 405 I saw Carole Spangler, standing on the parkway. For the first time I truly appreciated her service. A carpool companion would shave an hour off my last commute.

She was in a poor humor. She had started back down south with a guy who "assumed oral sex was included."

"What did you do?"

"I don't think much of that question."

"I mean, how did you extricate yourself from the situation?"

She shrugged. "I was surprised. I almost pulled my Facer, but I didn't think it would fool him. I told him to let me out or I'd yank the wheel. He pulled over back there."

"I don't think this setup is right for you," I said. "You get too much of a cross section. You should ride with Harry."

"He's not that much better. Just sappier. All men are pigs." She paused. "My dad was all right."

I thought I'd put in a farewell word for Harry. Carole seemed unaware of the idealistic nature of his feeling for her.

"Men have a pig *side*," I amended, "because we're biologically vulnerable to attractive women. But see, Harry's an exception. He's *had* the babes. He was married to two cover girls."

"He's had the best, now he wants the rest."

"No. He thinks you're special. He looks at you the way the rest of us look at the babes. No offense."

She watched the traffic for a moment.

"After Kevin left me, I swore, next guy takes advantage of me, I'm gonna kill him. Then your friend Harry throws me in his jeep like a sack of empties. Testing my vow." She shook her head. "I missed my time, though. I could've done it right then, that day. But now I can't. He's too . . . I don't know. Preposterous."

"Well, I guess, in a way. But he's sincere."

She made a quick finger-down-the-throat gesture—whether in response to my sentiment or to Harry himself, I couldn't tell. A discouraging signal, at best.

About a minute or two later she scrunched around in the passenger seat to face me. She wore a conspiratorial look.

"You know what would shake him up? You and me. On that long table when he gets home. Huh? Me and his right-hand gofer."

"Oh ho-ho," I agreed politely.

She stared at me.

"Your face is turning red," she said.

"Well, yours should be too," I said, annoyed. "He's trying to make amends to you for what he did."

She flung herself back in her seat and faced front again.

"You're afraid of him," she said.

"Afraid of *you*," I muttered.

"You're his parrot. You sit on his shoulder and he feeds you by hand."

"Actually, today was my last feeding."

Peripherally I saw her head swivel back toward me.

"You really quit? I never thought you'd go through with it. You're a weekly paycheck guy."

"Give me a month. I'll look like I never got a paycheck in my life."

. . .

Laguna's Main Beach features a curving boardwalk, a basketball court, and volleyball in the sand. For a week I went to Main Beach every day. I went in the ocean, something I hadn't done for ten years. It was bracing. Chilly, though. Daylight savings time ended. I thought of going back to Illinois for the holidays, but I didn't want to go home unemployed. Mom still hadn't recovered from my return from college.

It didn't feel like a new life yet; it felt like a vacation. I didn't miss anyone from work except Joanne, and even that had a bright side: I didn't see her with Fairbanks anymore.

But I missed Where Did They Go? That was my baby. I had always tried to make reference to something you wouldn't be likely to recall or know about the subject, like Ted Bessell's work on *It's a Man's World.* Stuff that would otherwise be lost.

One night I saw Reuben drinking in the Barnacle Room near Main Beach. I joined him for a beer. He had cash, and was wearing his London Fog coat. Despite his new affluence he didn't seem peppy. I asked him how things were going and he said, "The way I knew they'd go."

Harry was assisting Carole Spangler in the administration of Carpool Companions. They'd taken on Paul, Donna, Stevie and Lorenzo as employees and given each of them a sign, an orange baseball cap and a cell phone so they could call Reuben at head-quarters—Harry's house—all day and report the license number of the vehicles they were getting into. Then at the end of rush hour, when they got back to town, they'd pay Reuben the company's percentage of the ride fees.

"It's getting all organized," I observed.

"Oh yeah," agreed Reuben. He drank his beer. "Harry wants us to get licensed."

When I asked about Carole, he said, "I don't know, he's taking her up and back now. I'm dispatcher. I stay home."

"So Carole's with Harry now?"

"Beats me. There's so many rooms, I don't know where the hell she's at. I got half a mind to move out. He's got these losers all over the place."

The Friday after I quit, Harry had the first of his accidents. I would have missed it if I hadn't attended the high school football game, partway up the hill toward Top of the World.

The Laguna football team deserved all the support it could get. The school was small and the players were usually outweighed, outnumbered and overwhelmed by the bigger schools in their conference. My neighbor Ginny's son Cody DeVoe, who had walked Sashi for me after school for years while I was at *Who's Hot,* played fullback and linebacker on the varsity at 145 pounds, which will give you some idea. On kickoffs he'd get run over and flattened, cartoonlike. But he was resilient; he'd pop right back up, also cartoonlike, and follow the play. One time he sneezed four hours after a game and dirt came out of his nose.

On this Friday night Cody and his teammates were down 30 points in the second period when Harry's dog Savage ran across the field, to cheers. Harry was nowhere to be seen. When Savage reached the near sideline I came down out of the bleachers and called him. He bounded over agreeably enough. I heard the sound of sirens, heading up the hill. I convinced Savage to follow me to my car and drove up Park—one of the two steep winding roads which lead to the Top of the World.

Harry's castle was a block to the left once I got to the top. By the time I arrived his east wing had burned down. The fire was pretty much out. There was a fire station less than a mile down Harry's street, and another engine had come up from downtown. Both engines were in the semicircular driveway. The guest, or burned, wing was a busted-in shell, soaked and charred and smoking. The center and west sections were untouched. There were no Santa Ana winds that night, so the flames hadn't blown anywhere.

They had aroused the neighbors considerably, though. As I pulled up, there were several people out in the street, along with the firefighters. The homeowners surrounded Harry and Carole Spangler. The rest of Harry's guest roster—Reuben, Lorenzo and the others—was gathered in the driveway, watching the firemen tromping in and out of the east wing.

The neighbors had a lot to say. Harry's open-door policy had caused resentment even before the fire. Top of the World was an upscale neighborhood, and Harry's new policy had lowered the tone. Folks had been leaving little notes on his windshield and his doorstep, telling him it was a misdemeanor to house the homeless without a permit.

Harry had responded, and was responding now, that he wasn't housing the homeless; he was entertaining guests. Now he was jawing with the main neighborhood spokesperson, a thin, intense woman named Barsky.

"This is pretty outrageous," she was telling him. "It's not like we haven't had enough fire around here. Everybody knows you've been bringing these people in, and now they're dropping lit cigarettes or whatever."

"Wasn't me," Carole Spangler told the woman coolly. "When I pass out with a lit cigarette I pee on it and put it out."

My arrival with Savage occasioned a joyous reunion between man and dog at the foot of the driveway. Harry hugged Savage ferociously and followed by hugging me.

"He wasn't in the laundry room; I didn't know where to look." He pulled back to look me in the eye. "This is the best thing you've ever done."

Damn, I thought. That's probably true.

After that it got nearly as heated in the street as it had been in Harry's east wing. Ms. Barsky got up in Harry's face about his guests, and Harry responded with some dark speculation about how the fire could have been started by a neighbor wanting to "frame" them. Then up came Reuben with a new theory.

"One working smoke alarm in the whole wing," he told Harry. "I just found out. You know what I think?"

"No, but I'll bet it's good," said Harry.

"I think you lured us up here to burn us all up. Genocide."

While the debate continued, I sidled over to Carole Spangler and asked her what had happened. She nodded toward Ms. Barsky.

"That bitch ought to be on the psychic network."

"Whaddya mean? Cigarette? It's a little early to be falling asleep with a cigarette."

Carole lowered her voice.

"Not for Lorenzo."

I looked around and spotted Lorenzo, sitting on the curb beside the foot of the driveway in a ratty old coat, glancing up at the firemen now and then through his stringy hair.

On this evening, Carole said, Harry had invited the Carpool Companions into the ballroom/theater in the west wing to watch a new Bill Murray video on his big screen. Everyone had attended except Lorenzo, who had remained in the east end, following his practice of leaving lit smokes on flat surfaces and going into whatever new rooms his voices were coming from.

"He's like Johnny Appleseed," she said. "He burned down his last two apartments. On one of 'em the landlord got a whole new building out of it and gave him his security deposit back."

Eventually, the source of the blaze was indeed traced to one of Lorenzo's discarded Salems. But Harry didn't kick him out. He was so dedicated to his dream of *Second Chances* that he was willing to hand out third and fourth ones. In his new vision, there seemed to be no such thing as a bad boy. He simply required Lorenzo to stop smoking in the house, and Lorenzo left voluntarily.

Harry moved his remaining guests into the west wing and carried on, despite protests from his neighbors, despite being dropped by his insurance carrier, despite losing consecutive housekeepers who balked at picking up after everyone. He swept criticism and obstacles aside, like a fool or a visionary.

· · ·

Every fall Harry hosted a company picnic at his home, and this year it took place a week after and in spite of the fire. I was invited, but I didn't attend. I didn't want to haunt it.

This time I didn't hear the sirens go up the hill. I didn't know what happened until the following Monday, when Peter Hood called me from work and said Harry was at Mission Medical Center, south of Laguna.

"Harry'd like you to come see him," he said. "He's going to be okay. We were scared there for a while."

When I entered Harry's hospital room I got a jolt. He was looking up at the TV, watching Montel Williams in a glazed, slack-jawed kind of way. He had a tag on his wrist and was hooked up to an IV bottle. His glasses were off, which always made him look weaker. He seemed powerless.

"How are you?" I asked him.

His head flopped toward me. His eyes cleared. He was weak, not drugged.

"Oh, I'm fine. They're filling me up with regular."

"What happened?"

"Well, we *say* we got a bad piece of tuna, but we find it curious that we are the only guy who got one."

I sat down beside the bed and we watched TV while he told me the story in blips—short sentences. Most of the staff had shown up for the picnic, if only to eat at Harry's expense. The only absentees were Jimmy Nations, who didn't trust his car to get down to Laguna and back up north to L.A., and a couple people from the TV end. Ted Fairbanks attended with Joanne. And Harry's Second Chancers were also on hand. There'd been a varied selection of food, provided by caterers, on several picnic tables in

Harry's huge backyard. Ribs, burgers and hot dogs for the carnivores; salads and pastas for the more fastidious.

"I got this tuna salad from a big bowl on the table. Put some on my plate. Took a phone call. Talked to some people. Came back to my plate. Ate my salad. Then I'm showing the east wing to everybody, and my throat is all . . . constricted. And I'm nauseous. You know? Then, at the same time, stomach cramps so bad, I swear I thought the Alien was in there. I'm down in the grass, screaming, moaning, swearing . . . worst possible language. I called for Carole. She sat with me till the paramedics came. She wouldn't come in the ambulance though. My gut hurt so bad I asked the paramedics to throw me out the back."

"Well, what was it? You're allergic to tuna?"

"No. Scombroid poisoning."

"How do you spell that?"

"Scombroid. Who cares?"

"That's not the print media spirit, Harry."

He looked at me accusingly.

"What's it to you? You quit. You abandoned me. Now here I am."

"It's my fault?"

"It's somebody's fault."

"The caterers?"

Harry shook his head peevishly.

"They couldn't know what I'd eat. But the people at work, they know I've been off red meat and eating seafood because I've been ordering it in when we'd work late. And the rest of the tuna salad was fine. Just the tuna salad *on my plate*. Get it? Somebody from the office did it while I was walking around. I told 'em, 'Try and stop me.' Remember?"

He picked up his clicker and channel-surfed, while I stared blankly at the screen.

"You don't believe that," I said.

He just kept clicking.

"Why couldn't it have been somebody in your new group?" I asked.

"They have no reason."

He finally stopped clicking, back on Montel.

"Well, if you're really worried," I said, "you should talk to the cops. Or hire bodyguards. Food tasters."

Harry shook his head again.

"It makes the office situation seem chaotic. I can't have that right now. I want to address this unobtrusively." He regarded me. "Through you. You know everybody. You can come back—just temporarily—slither around, use your nitpicky brain, find out which of 'em did it." Before I could speak, he added, "I'll match your severance payout."

His last sentence obscured the one before it for a moment, but I finally refocused.

"I don't think any of them did it," I said. "And even if you're right . . . why can't you figure it out yourself? You're the genius."

Harry spoke pontifically, to the ceiling.

"Sometimes a dwarf on a giant's shoulders can see farther than the giant can."

I was speechless for a moment.

"Was that from your desk calendar?" I asked finally.

"No, the *Great Thoughts* book."

"Well, it's pretty goddamn irritating."

Harry raised a hand apologetically.

"I'm sorry. I'm not myself."

"Hell you're not."

"Well, I'm not happy, then." He looked hurt. "Carole didn't visit me. I had to call *her*, to tell her I was gonna survive. She goes, 'They said the symptoms usually subside within twelve hours.' She didn't trouble herself to come by."

"Well, I don't know why you're surprised. I mean, there's somebody who's given some *thought* to doing you in. What about her?"

"She'd never poison me. She has some feeling for me. She just has a hard time expressing it." He moved onto his side, to face me. "C'mon. Be my friend. Double severance. How about it? You got other offers? You don't need money? Got your retirement all set up?"

He was touching a sore point: I was concerned about savings. But I thought his theory was rubbish. From my dwarf's, or parrot's, position on his shoulder, all I could see was unintentional food poisoning. Also, I didn't care for his use of the word "slither" to indicate what he wanted me to do.

"I'm gonna decline, Harry. I think you just got a piece of accidental tuna."

His eyes narrowed.

"Do I deserve to die?" he asked suddenly.

I was taken aback.

"Why are you hesitating?" he demanded. "You shouldn't have to think about that."

"No," I said, "you don't deserve to die. But I don't think anybody's trying to kill you."

"Oh, yeah? You should see 'em at the office. They won't even look me in the eye, except for your old pal Joanne, who bitches all day about her workload and who missed half a dozen typos in the millennium issue."

"Well, you're making her do too much. Did you make her do Where Did They Go too?"

"No. I'm discontinuing it."

I blinked at him.

"What?"

"The feature's a waste of time. I only ever did it as a favor to you."

I exhaled, and stood up.

"I'd like another shot at that deserve-to-die question."

We stared at each other coldly.

"Thanks for dropping by," he said.

I went to the door and turned, nearly colliding with a nurse coming in.

"In discontinuing Where Did They Go," I said with dignity, "you are obliterating the last trace of perspective in your magazine."

"So speaks the dwarf," said Harry.

NINE

Two days later I came home from the beach to find I had a message from Emily Hahn on my machine:

"Have you figured it out yet? Shame on you if you haven't."

I rummaged through my box of personal scraps from the office and came upon the piece of paper Emily had given me—the one with the E-mail gibberish from John Easter's man, Wesley Willis.

;pd smhr;rd mpb yrm

I stared at the letters. They looked strangely familiar, as they had when I first saw them. But I didn't know why until I gave up and dropped the paper beside my computer keyboard.

One of my first great triumphs at the magazine was deciphering a similar piece of nonsense sent to us by a Pulitzer Prize–winning columnist named Jim Olaf. Harry had hired him for a one-shot article for prestige purposes, and Olaf had transmitted the piece from his home computer in New York on deadline and then gone out drinking. Right in the middle of the column was half a line of meaningless garble, much like what I was looking at now. And I had figured out that Olaf, while typing it, had momentarily been distracted or interrupted and put his fingers down one key over on the keyboard for a few words. So instead of typing, for instance, "the screening was a disaster," he had typed "yjr dvtrrmomh esd s fodsdyrt"—a crucial difference in meaning.

After I allowed for that one key over on the letters in front of me, I sat and stared at it for a minute or two. Then the phone rang.

"It says 'Los Angeles Nov ten,' " said Emily when I said hi.

"How do you know?" I asked. "You gave it to me. What'd you do, write it down twice?"

"I most certainly did. I wasn't going to depend on you. He's meeting Easter next week."

"Not much of a message," I said. "I was hoping we could clear up that JFK thing."

"Not much of a code, either," she said. "Anybody who's typed all her life is gonna get that one eventually."

"Well, they just did it so you couldn't read it right off the screen over his shoulder," I said.

"I haven't seen any more. I guess it doesn't matter. He's gonna sell it and we're gonna be out. I could just kill him."

Emily had a right to be upset. She had expected to stay with *Who's Hot* until retirement. But she wasn't old enough to retire and she was too old to get rolling again somewhere else.

"I'm used to Harry," she said. "But I can't start all over again putting up with another one."

"I guess we all did too well," I told her. "We made the place too attractive."

"Yeah." There was a short pause. "Harry's in today; he's coming down the hall. You want to talk to him?"

"No, we're kinda . . ."

"You know . . ." Emily lowered her voice. "Joanne doesn't seem so happy with anchor boy lately."

"No?"

"She says he's self-centered beyond the acceptable level. You should call her."

"I don't beg, Emily. It doesn't work."

"Well, I'm taking her to lunch tomorrow, 'cause she's been working so hard. Come up coincidentally and I'll invite you out with us. Spur of the moment."

"Well, if I can. I got a whole new life going here."

· · ·

It was actually nice, driving up north. I didn't leave until 10:30, so traffic was light for California. And I wasn't late for work, because I couldn't be. I couldn't picture Joanne dropping Ted Fairbanks and switching back to me, but Emily seemed to think she was dissatisfied, and it gave point to the day.

The first person I saw when I got to the office was Carole Spangler, scanning the covers on the wall in the reception area. She tossed me a glance but didn't say hi, so I didn't either. Behind her, Bobbi LaMott raised perfect eyebrows at the sight of me.

"Are you coming back?" she asked.

"I came back to tell you I've gotten taller."

She smiled, pushed her chair back and stood.

"See?" I said, ignoring the evidence.

"I thought at first you were trying to get your job back," she said. "I'm glad you're not. Everyone admires you for getting out. You're like *The Shawshank Redemption*."

"Well, thank you, Bobbi." It was the most dramatic role she'd ever seen me in.

Joanne came down the hall. I sensed her coming but didn't look at her until she got close.

"What are you doing here?" she asked.

"Came to see Bobbi. You don't think I came up here to drool over you, drool you? Do you? How are you? You look good."

I hadn't seen her in a week and a half. Actually she looked thinner, and a little haggard around the eyes. But she still looked good. She had a considerable distance to drop before she wouldn't look good.

"Well, final read sucks," she said. "And I suck at it."

"Did you do it out loud?" I asked.

"No. I was self-conscious."

"There's where you went wrong. You've got to sing out. Make some noise."

"You want me to make noise."

"Well, I just think you'll do better if you read audibly. I used to—"

At this point there was a deafening, animal yell from the end of the hall, from Harry's office . . . from Harry. It was part roar, part scream. A kind of "RRRRAAAAAHHHHHHHHH!" And as it ended, Harry appeared in his doorway, suddenly, with both hands shot out to the doorframe, as if he'd been thrown. He stood there, arms and legs apart, star-shaped, in his shorts and T-shirt. His hair was in the mad scientist style. He emitted another howling roar. Emily Hahn, sitting at her desk outside the door to his right, shrank back from him.

"BASTARDS!" he bellowed. "That's it! Conference room!"

"What's the matter?" I called down to him. "What happened?"

"Oh," he said, seeing me. "Mr. Accident! I'll tell you: I just had another one! I had a BIG one!"

"Wow," said Joanne. "Is that smoke coming off him?"

. . .

I had a childhood friend who lived on a farm outside Bloomington. His parents had built a little detached semishack in some trees out near their cornfield, and this shack, although it had no walls, had a refrigerator, which got current from the main farmhouse via a series of extension cords. All the pickers kept their soda and water in this fridge during the day. I was out there one afternoon when we had a sudden electrical storm, and I got the opportunity to see what happens when lightning hits a refrigerator while a friend is leaning up against its door.

What happens is, the friend goes hurtling out of the shack as if two giants are carrying him by the arms and lands several yards away on his face. He lives, but he's changed.

After twenty minutes on the Cardiac Rider and twenty more on his new Versa Climber, Harry had flopped into his office recliner to use one of the four massage capabilities—Japanese, Chinese, Swedish and Ultimate—and pressed his clicker. Whereupon he'd been flung through space, from his chair to the doorway. It turned out that part of the vinyl covering down near the crease between seat and back had been torn, exposing some of the wiring. When Harry set his controls for Ultimate, he got a massive power surge to the spine.

As we all filed into the conference room, he stood in the hallway, staring at each face as it passed. His own face was clammy. He was obviously eager to talk. He was rubbing his hands together. His head quivered slightly now and then, in a kind of shiver. He could barely wait until we all got inside. When Steve Kluszewski and Jimmy Nations came through as the last men in, Harry followed, slammed the door and turned to address the staff.

"That was a good one," he told us. "That was a dandy. But you've failed again. I'm still standing."

"What are you talking about?" asked Jimmy, leaning against the far wall.

"Well, Jimmy, I'm talking about my recliner. I just sat back in it to look through a copy of *Buzz* and I got a little buzz myself. I went across my office without using my feet."

"Harry, you should go to the ER—you might be in shock."

This observation was made by Emily Hahn, who drew a stare from Harry.

"Is that a witticism? 'Shock'?" he demanded. "Because I'm not in the mood. I've read Marvel comics where guys became supervillains from what just happened to me." He held out his hands and stared at his fingertips. "I want to know," he said deliberately, "who fucked with my chair."

There was a pause while Harry looked around. I did too,

searching for tells. I was unsuccessful, though. A roomful of people who have every right to look concerned and uneasy don't give away much when they look that way. Even Carole Spangler looked a little worried as she stood against the near wall.

"I should fire you all," he said finally. "No. I should make you all sit in the chair. We could have a distance-traveled contest. When I find out who did it, I'll be calling you back into this room to witness punishment. We'll do it the way they used to do it at sea." He walked around the table, slowly, staring into everyone's face, talking as he went. "Do you think you've struck a blow for labor by doing this? Because you haven't. Anybody can kill a boss. But that's not winning the argument. You can't do it anyway. I defy you to kill me. You can't. Because I haven't fulfilled my destiny. And I'm ready for you now. If I was a dummy, I wouldn't be able to pay my ex-wife a hundred thousand dollars a month." He quivered as he said this. "From now on, a new dress code. You guys wear whatever you want, and I'll wear explosives strapped to my chest. If I fall, I'll take you all with me. This woman right here"—by now he had reached Carole and put his arm around her shoulder—"can turn the world on with her smile." He hugged her to his side. "The irony is that you were all going to get bicycles, and you didn't know it. When I was a kid, if I was bad, my mother would always say, 'I was going to get you a bicycle, but now you've done this, so I won't.' That used to make me crazy. But now, I can tell you, I was going to get you all bicycles, but now you've done this, so I won't."

Eden Ramos caught my eye. "911," she mouthed, tilting her head toward Harry.

I started for the door. Harry spotted me.

"Where you goin'?" he demanded.

I looked around.

"Lunch," I said.

"You'll stay here with everybody else," said Harry.

"I can do what I want, Elektro. I don't work here anymore."

I got out the door before Harry could respond and ran to Emily's desk, the closest. As I picked up the phone, Harry emerged from the conference room, holding Carole Spangler by the hand.

"Who are you calling?" he asked suspiciously.

"Uhh. . . ." I felt caught, guilty.

"Lunch," said Harry. "Good idea. C'mon."

He walked down the hall in his T-shirt and shorts.

.   .   .

Harry wouldn't get into my vehicle, and I wouldn't get into his unless he let me drive. It was a standoff until Harry admitted he was a bit light-headed. So we ended up with me behind the wheel of his jeep. I drove us west, toward the 405. Harry was still a little sweaty. Carole sat lengthwise in the backseat, smoking.

"We'll go to lunch," he said. "Then we'll go back and hook up every last one of those assholes to a polygraph. We'll hook the assholes' *ass*holes to a polygraph."

"Maybe the chair got damaged in the paintball fight," I said. "Is that possible?"

"It was something." Harry spoke in a kind of wonderment. "The power of electricity. That's why they always strapped the killers down before they executed 'em. Because if you didn't, as soon as they got the juice, they'd go right through the wall. They'd escape."

"Harry, I'm gonna take you to the ER."

"No, you're taking us to lunch. That's a word that sounds like food. It sounds lunchy and munchy. 'Food' also sounds like food."

"Harry—"

"I'm fine. The whole episode cleaned out my system. That current scraped out my arteries and platelets and cholesterol; it's all gone. I'm streamlined. Completely flushed. If they could calculate the correct therapeutic voltage, they could shoot it through old people and rejuvenate them. Take the freeway south, I want to go to Giorgio's; they're informal."

We got on the 405. Harry was in good spirits, and while his conversation didn't inspire confidence, it wasn't that far removed from the way he usually thought. I figured I'd keep an eye on him and if he showed any signs of weakening or seizing up I'd go to the nearest trauma center.

It was hot. October and November can occasionally get pretty toasty in southern California. I was unused to Harry's jeep, but I liked it. There was good air circulation.

The only thing I couldn't figure out was the gauges. They were so much more unstable than mine. For instance, on my car, and every other I'd ever driven, you never saw the gas gauge in motion. But on Harry's jeep, the arrow moved visibly, from right to left, from F toward E.

"Your gas gauge broken?" I asked finally as we zipped along in the carpool lane.

"That's a little personal," said Harry. "I told you I'm fine."

"No, I mean your arrow here." I pointed at the dash. "It's moving. Is it disconnected?"

"The hell you talkin' about? Everything works on this vehicle."

"Well, in that case it really eats fuel."

Carole Spangler leaned forward and looked over my shoulder to see what I was talking about.

"We're losing altitude," she said.

It was a disturbing sight. I'd never seen such a thing. The arrow was perceptibly moving, to the left.

Harry leaned over too, and looked at it.

"Wow. Why is it doing that?" he asked.

"Maybe it's broken," suggested Carole.

I wanted her to be right. This was very unnerving. I'd faced many a predicament on the road—I'd had flat tires and blown radiator caps; once a surfboard blew off the roof of the car in front of me and came whirling back past my windshield—but I'd never seen a gas gauge that went down like an old elevator arrow.

I was uncomfortable in the carpool lane, way over on the left. "If we're spilling gas," I said, "I don't want to be here."

Traffic was heavy, but moving quickly. I didn't have time to wait for the lane line to break, so I just signaled a turn, sped up, picked a spot, veered to the right and hoped for the best. This is the one freeway maneuver, of course, that above all others endangers and enrages your fellow drivers. If it doesn't lead to a fatal accident, it can easily lead to a fatal confrontation, especially in California. As I crossed five lanes in an attempt to make the next off-ramp, I heard and saw things behind me—screaming, swerving, skidding, screeching—which made the perspiration break out pretty freely. Also, the swerving and braking made it difficult for me to gauge the gaps.

In this instance the phase I'd been going through since breaking up with Joanne—the period of relative unconcern about my personal safety—helped me, because otherwise I don't think I'd've been able to cut across like that. I timed my veers and found my gaps and made it to the off-ramp, crossing the gravelly separator just beyond the lane fork.

The ramp curved up and to the right, and I followed it, hoping for a service station on the first corner. The gas arrow was coming down to E.

"Jesus," said Carole Spangler behind me. She was looking back toward the freeway. "I could see their faces."

"What's next, a wheelie?" asked Harry.

"Shut up."

There was a gas station at the first light, all right, but it was abandoned, and the station building itself was gutted. I pulled in anyway, turned off the ignition and slumped back in my seat. Carole sat forward, looking over my shoulder at the gauge.

"Ground floor," she said.

We all got out and walked around behind the jeep. A stream of gasoline coursed onto the concrete and flowed back down toward the gutter.

"This is so unsafe," I said.

"Sabotage," said Harry flatly.

We walked over to the sidewalk. Off-ramp traffic went past. Fortunately, none of the drivers I'd cut off had been able to make the exit. That's when most of the shootings occur.

Carole was still smoking, which I thought was foolhardy.

"The cigarette," I told her.

Reaching over, Harry took it out of her mouth and flicked it into the street. It landed in the trail of gasoline and burst into flame. The flame followed our gas trail back up the driveway and across the station's concrete pavement until it reached Harry's jeep, where it encountered the fumes from the gas tank and blew it up.

We all recoiled, flinching from the blast. Then we watched the jeep burn. Of the three of us, Carole was the only one to laugh.

TEN

I'm accident-prone myself. I hit my head on the freezer door pretty regularly. I slip, trip, stub and bonk. One time I was reading a paper while strolling down the street and walked right into a bus stop bench.

But as we stood on the sidewalk in front of the abandoned gas station and the burning jeep, I saw that I wasn't in Harry Poe's league. Harry wasn't safe in his house, he wasn't safe in his jeep, he wasn't safe in his chair. He stood, now, in his shorts and his T-shirt, gazing pensively while his jeep interior, along with his custom tennis racket and his earthquake survival kit, melted before his eyes.

After a session with police and firefighters, we got a ride back to *Who's Hot* from two cops who speculated that our "fuel fill line" had come loose in some way. It was hard to tell with the jeep in its present condition.

I thought that Harry would ask the police to question the staff about the fuel fill line, or that he'd grill everybody himself, but he said no, not today. He just wanted to go south and think. All he did at the office was put his street clothes back on, while Carole and I waited for him in the reception area. Then we went out to my car, where there was a brief argument about driving again. Harry had the sensational nerve to tell me he didn't like the way I'd handled the jeep. I responded that I hadn't cared for the way he disposed of Carole's cigarette.

I drove. Carole sat in the back again, giggling occasionally and saying, "FWOOM." I stayed in the middle lane, my eyes darting to the gas gauge every few seconds.

Harry didn't speak all the way down to Laguna Beach. I didn't blame him. He'd had quite a series of mishaps. His head whipped to the side once, when a motorcyclist came up fast on the right.

Harry, however, had a sense of his own destiny which seemed to insulate him. He was brooding when he got in the car; he emerged cheerful, with a new resolve, in the parking lot of the Hotel Laguna. He had chosen our destination. He wanted to sit down in a place that wouldn't burn down, blow up or short out.

We sat on the hotel's restaurant terrace, overlooking beach and ocean. Recovered from his scombroid poisoning and no longer feeling ill effects from his electrocution, Harry ordered calamari tacos. Carole and I chose chicken. He told the waitress that he and Carole would be on one check and I would be on another, explaining to me that money was a bit tight right now and he needed to be frugal; he meant nothing personal by it.

As the waitress left, Harry took his memo pen out of his jacket pocket and spoke into it: "Leave office door unlocked as usual, but install security camera." He put the pen back in his pocket and looked at me.

"Do you use your pen?" he asked.

I hung my head a little. Harry looked mildly sad.

"How about your accident theory?" he inquired. "That still holding up?"

We looked down at the beach. Kids were skimboarding. I could see a sandpiper hopping along, in and out of the surf, pecking industriously. An older guy with a metal detector walked south to north.

"I've got a meeting coming up," said Harry, "and at this rate, I'm not going to be able to attend. By the way, did Emily decipher that E-mail from Wesley Willis on her own or did you help her?"

I didn't goggle, or drop anything, but my face got hot, and Harry waved it off.

"Forget it. I'm the dumbass who left it up on the screen. At the time it was minor gamesmanship. But I know Emily told everybody about that message. And I think somebody decided they really don't want me to make that meeting."

"These are people we *know,* Harry," I protested. "We're not the Corleones."

Harry nodded. "I have to make a call," he said.

He walked back into the building and through the bar, toward the phones. The waitress arrived. Carole and I ate our chicken and looked out at the ocean, which glinted especially brightly this afternoon.

Carole's only beverage was water. She caught me watching her take a sip.

"I don't have time to drink right now," she said. "Someday I'll get my own place. And it'll have a bar in the den. I'll go in every Friday and come out Monday."

We concentrated on our food for a few moments.

"Who do you think's doing all this to Harry?" I asked after a while.

"Maybe he's doing it to himself," she said casually. "He blew up the jeep." She sat back and returned my gaze. "It isn't me. I'm not that cold. If he'd been in the jeep when it blew up, I wouldn't have laughed."

Harry eventually returned, sat down, snapped his napkin authoritatively and said, "It's set." He attacked his taco and spoke between chews: "We're going to London day after tomorrow. I had to work it out with Easter. I was gonna leave a message—it's like two in the morning there—but he's up. He's 'jamming.' Can you stand it? The guy plays guitar. You'd think you could get him ripped and then take him for millions, but nobody's ever done it."

"I'm sorry: Go back to the 'we're,' " I said. "The 'we're' going.' "

"The three of us. Instead of here on the tenth, we'll meet him there, on the ninth. The ninth, get it? Lucky. You'll get a kick out of Easter. It's like he's just this side of a piss drunk, but he never makes a mistake. And he loves the magazine. I talked to him at a banquet out here. You know what he said just now? He said I was the only genius he met in California."

"You believed that?" asked Carole.

Harry raised an index finger.

"Sometimes a bullshitter tells the truth, just to cleanse his palate."

"Is that from the *Great Thoughts* book?" I asked, impressed.

"No, that's mine." He looked at Carole. "I'm gonna get the money for *Second Chances*, and you're gonna be in the first issue. You've got a passport, right? Didn't you tell me once, your parents took you to England or Ireland?"

Carole blinked.

"My dad took me to the James Herriot country," she said. "All creatures great and small." To my astonishment, tears suddenly appeared in her eyes.

"You okay?" I asked.

She wiped the tears away impatiently.

"Because I loved the stories and I thought I wanted to be a vet. Mom was in a play, so he just took me. We went to London too. The West End." She blew her nose in her napkin. "But later I changed my mind about being a vet. It looked too hard. I was too lazy."

"Did your dad say that?" Harry asked.

"My dad," she said slowly, "told me I could do anything."

"Well," said Harry mildly, after a moment, "maybe we can stay over after the meeting and sightsee."

"I got a business to run," she said.

"Let Reuben do it for a week," said Harry. "All he does is bitch about how he doesn't get to do enough. Come on. You've started a business out of nothing and gotten it rolling. Take a break."

Carole wiped her nose again.

"What do you get out of it?" she asked.

"I like your conversation," declared Harry. "I never know what you're gonna say."

She sighed.

"I'd have to be able to go wherever I want," she said. "And an expense allowance equal to what I could make here."

"Absolutely," agreed Harry. "Establish your conditions. That's great." He looked at me. "See how she cuts through to basics? She's got a mind like a drill."

"And a room of my own. No ménage à trois. Or deux, either."

"Oh, hell no," he said irritably. "Why touch?" He transferred his attention to me. "I know *you've* got a passport from when we went to that film awards ceremony."

"What do you need me for?" I asked.

"Human shield."

I shook my head. "I don't think . . ."

"Look," said Harry, "Easter says no lawyers, just man-to-man. But he'll have *his* people around. It's his turf. It's bad enough he can buy me a hundred times and not feel it. I need a second. Who else can I take? Come on, you turned me down for the other thing, you gotta step up now. I'll pay your freight and a consultant's fee."

I shifted uncomfortably and said, "I don't know . . ."

Harry sat back and stared at me.

"You know, you're yankin' me off a little bit here. What don't you know?"

"Well . . . about the staff."

I hadn't wanted to bring it up. I knew he wouldn't like it.

"What about them?" he said quietly.

"I know you're a little down on 'em right now," I said slowly. "But they've done decent work for you. . . . I think you should get some kind of assurance from Easter that he'll either keep 'em or give 'em a severance package. Granted, there's—there may be a bad one in there somewhere, but even if that's true, I don't think they should all suffer."

Harry dabbed at his mouth with his napkin.

"If you want me to discuss staff with John Easter," he said, "you can friggin' well come along and see that I do. Otherwise, I might forget, and that's a promise." The lazy left eye was down a bit as he dropped his napkin on his plate, sat back and regarded me impassively. "You always want to do things right. Let me ask you something. Do you think it's right, what's happening to me?"

I thought it over.

"Okay," I said, after a moment. "I'll go. But we'll probably disagree about everything."

"I don't care. At least your face won't change."

"What?"

Harry surveyed the horizon.

"Remember when we did acid and watched *Invasion of the Body Snatchers*?"

Well, yes, I did. It was one of the most horrifying evenings of my life. While at college in our idiot youth, Harry and I had split a tab as an experiment and gone to the school auditorium to watch Don Siegel's landmark film. During the climactic scene, amid a raucous, enthusiastic crowd, as Dana Wynter revealed herself to Kevin McCarthy as a pod person from outer space, I had turned to my right and come face-to-face with Harry, who was now wearing a melting mask of pulsating cartilage and bulging eyeballs. In twin paroxysms of terror and revulsion, we had clawed our way to opposite aisles and out of the theater.

"After I got my shock in the recliner," Harry told me now, "I looked at those people in the conference room . . . they were all Body Snatchers. Everybody was a pod except you two."

. . .

I didn't hear from Harry the next day; he was on the move, pre-
paring paperwork for the trip and doing some banking. In the
evening I gave Sashi an extra long walk, guilty in advance for
leaving her. She was to stay with Savage while we were gone, and
Harry was arranging for daily walks from Scoop Troop, but I believed she'd still miss me. She'd quickly grown accustomed to my
being home more.

As she and I returned from our walk, coming down the curve
of Wilson Terrace, with the house up ahead, I thought I saw
Joanne, sitting on the front steps under the porch light. She lived
way up in Manhattan Beach, though, and I'd mistaken other
women for her two or three times since we'd broken up. I was
curious to see who she would turn out to be this time. I was
shocked when we reached the yard and it was herself.

Sashi was delighted to see her, and I guess I gamboled about
in front of her a little myself, until I found out why she'd come.
I'd been daydreaming about such a miracle for a long time. We let
her in and she walked around the living room, her hands in the
pockets of her long tan overcoat. It had been a much cooler day
and evening, and she wore a little tan cap; I believe it's called a
cloche. She always looked sweet in winter clothes. She saw my
suitcase, and the stuff piled in it. She saw the remains of my dinner
on the table in front of the couch.

"Still eating corned beef and Trix?"

"You act like they're on the same plate," I said defensively. "I
eat one first, then the other."

She turned to face me, tilting her head up imperiously at the
angle you hate to see.

"Payroll says Harry cut you a check."

"That's true," I acknowledged.

"So that was a charade, quitting. Harry had you pretend, for
some reason."

Joanne's habitual mistrust made this a tough charge to respond to. I decided to tell the truth, but I didn't have much confidence in it.

"Actually, no. I really quit. I'm just doing him a temporary favor. I'm gonna be a sidekick for a week."

"I thought you'd changed," she said. "But you're the same, aren't ya? Nice guy. A little wobbly. Company man."

"You came down here to *heckle* me?"

"No," she said, her head going up even higher. "I came down here to hear you deny it."

"Well, I do deny it. I'm quite a guy."

"Why are you packing?"

I hesitated. I'd promised Harry not to tell anyone when or where we were going.

"I'm going to Vegas to bet the Breeders' Cup."

"That explains the passport."

I sighed. It was sitting on top of the clothes in the suitcase. Joanne had such a quick eye; she could always spot the one thing that was wrong with this picture. She walked over and opened it up.

"U.K.," she remarked. "Harry's sending you to see John Easter?"

"Close enough," I said. "Now you must die."

She turned on me angrily.

"How can you take his side in this? He's trying to sell us all out."

"I guess I'm just a shit," I said.

"I guess so."

"Oh, THAT you believe."

She paced a bit. I knew there was little chance now of her believing anything I said for the rest of my life. I recalled a story she'd told me once, a family story about her toddlerhood. Apparently when she was little, her grandfather took his teeth out in front of her one day and shocked her into hysterics. She hadn't known such a thing was possible. For a long time after that she would reach into adults' mouths and feel around. She didn't trust anybody's teeth. And I knew that in her view now, after the incident of the passport, I was just a lot of bridgework.

I tried anyway.

"It happens I am going with Harry," I said, "but I'm going to try to influence the negotiations in the staff's favor."

This sounded like bullshit even to me.

"Whatever," said Joanne.

"Oh, great. Now you don't believe anything again. I told *one lie.* If one chair broke under you, would you stop sitting?"

"I'd stop sitting in that chair."

We stood around the room, looking this way and that. It was one of those scenes that resolves itself into a series of pauses, peppered by speeches whenever one of the parties thinks of a good one.

"All right," I said. "I'm going to tell you the exact truth as I understand it. I'm going partly for the sake of the staff, partly because I have nothing better to do and partly because I think Harry could use some backup."

"Oh, please."

"Okay. All right. Let me ask you something, Miss Oh Please. Are you one of those who thinks it's acceptable for a disgruntled employee to kill the boss? Because *I* think it's unprofessional."

"What are you talking about?"

"Scombroid poisoning and the electric chair."

"Oh, don't be so dramatic."

"You don't think it was dramatic when Harry took all that current?"

"I think it was an accident."

"Harry doesn't."

"Harry's paranoid."

"You know," I said thoughtfully, "for somebody like you,

who sees the adhesive under every hairpiece, it's odd that you don't see any possibility of foul play here."

She became indignant.

"Stop that beady look," she told me.

"I don't have a beady look."

"I beg your pardon. I know a beady look."

I jumped into a Gene Kelly howzat pose, and then dived into another silence. Joanne joined me. We studied the shelves, the walls, the floor.

"I better go," she said.

"Everything okay with Ted?"

"Fine."

"Anything wrong?"

"No."

"You must be pretty happy then."

"He's been coaching me," she said defiantly, "in anchor demeanor."

"Well, I think you'd be good without his coaching."

She bent down and petted Sashi. Then she straightened up and looked around the room one more time. We seemed to have hit the wall.

"It's none of my business what you do," she said. "I'm surprised you didn't say so."

She walked past me to the door.

"If you talk it up about Harry leaving," I said, "somebody might try to hit him before he can go."

"That's ridiculous," she said mechanically.

"Promise?"

She wouldn't turn around; she left without responding. For the rest of the night I thought of things I should have said.

• • •

Harry didn't tell me exactly when we were leaving; he just told me to be ready, and have Sashi ready to bring over. He didn't tell

Carole either. She seemed surprised, the following afternoon in the airport shuttle on the way up to LAX; she'd thought we were going later.

I think Harry was a little tense on the way up. There wasn't much conversation. Once we'd checked through the metal detector, though, he became exultant and euphoric. He laughed at the funnies in the *L.A. Times* while we ate in a Chinese restaurant near our gate. Then he called the office on his cell phone.

"Emily," he said, "if anyone wants to kill me I'll be in London."

ELEVEN

It's about nine hours from LAX to Heathrow, and we flew economy, a reflection of Harry's new frugality. In our Virgin Airlines fly-pak we got pencil, pad, socks, a sleep mask, comb, toothbrush, toothpaste and a shoehorn, plus a label to wear if you didn't want to be awakened for meals.

I can't sleep well on a plane anymore. When I was younger, and more limber, I could adjust myself to the contours of any seat. Now I'm only comfortable if I can stretch out. Harry, Carole and I were side by side by side in row 33, three seats against the window. To our left, across the aisle, was a near-miracle: five unoccupied center seats. All three of us noticed those five empty seats before takeoff. None of us said anything. But immediately after our early in-flight meal of steak and mushroom pie, Carole fought her way over me to get to them. She stretched out and slept throughout the flight, while I built up a sizeable dislike for her.

I was left with Harry. The in-flight movie selection wasn't much, and I'd only brought one book, because I planned to look for more in London. It was an English mystery, an Inspector Morse, and a good one, but it added to the discomfort of my seat. The general atmosphere of violence under what Reuben would have called its veneer of civility kept reminding me of our situation. Whenever we hit any turbulence I flinched; I kept expecting the plane to explode. Harry'd had no accidents for two days.

I skimmed his copy of the recently released millennium issue of *Who's Hot/Who's Not,* but I didn't really enjoy it. Harry kept pointing out Joanne's missed typos, for one thing. For another, any pleasures the Hot 99 had to offer were overshadowed by the Beatles-over-Christ climax, and although Peter Hood had managed a stylish kind of cubist, multicultural rendering of Jesus, it still seemed incongruous to me. Harry liked it. He was also proud of his Future Not list, which included Rush Limbaugh, Howard Stern, the cast of *Friends*, and Art Klee.

I looked at the masthead page—the first *WH/WN* I'd ever seen that didn't have me down as head goon. The list of staffers got me to speculating. I took up the pad and pencil supplied by the airline. At the top of each page I wrote the name of someone who might particularly dislike the idea of leaving *Who's Hot*.

Harry looked over to see what I was doing.

"Nancy Drew," he observed with approval. "Go ahead."

In no particular order, I went through the staff. Peter Hood cared for his aging mother, who was deteriorating mentally. Soon Peter would no longer be able to leave her at home while he worked, wouldn't be able to afford live-in care and would have to pay for assisted living indefinitely. I wrote down "Old mom."

Steve Kluszewski was still routinely intimidating coworkers. At the time I quit, he was upset about insurance. His wife's pleurisy had subsided and she was out of the hospital, but Steve was now paying bills, and that had made his disposition worse, if anything. The company's insurance was picking up 80 percent, but that left 20. There was nothing there worth killing over, to my way of thinking. But maybe not to Steve's. Below his name I wrote, "Temper."

Jimmy Nations had to be broke; I was sure of this because I had gone to the races with him. Jimmy's theory was that if you simply bet Gary Stevens every time he rode, you would come out ahead. This theory was erroneous. Not that Gary Stevens wasn't a great jock; it's just that he rode a lot of favorites, and all jockeys have periods during which they don't win much. Also, Jimmy liked to bet the "exotics"—Pick Six, trifectas, exactas, and so on. There are a few people who come out ahead doing this, but they are conscientious and studious. Jimmy was too impatient.

Beside Jimmy's name I wrote, "Out of the money."

"Do Bobbi LaMott," said Harry.

I gave a snort. Bobbi LaMott didn't need to tamper with cars and chairs and tuna. She was devastating enough on her own. Certainly she didn't need any particular job.

"Why?" I asked.

Harry shrugged. "We went out a couple times after Yasmine moved out. I—"

"Reason enough." I nodded, putting her name down with "Out with Harry" beside it.

Eden Ramos was entangled in a lawsuit, and had been for some time. Her teenage son had hit another car while driving hers. Eden's insurance had paid to the extent of her coverage; now the attorneys for the occupants of the other car wanted her house. "Lawyers," I wrote.

"Do Ernie," he said.

Ernie Scheffing was a highly motivated, intense, competitive salesman, but I didn't really know much about him.

"Wants to kill you because you beat him to work?"

"As a rule I like salesmen," Harry said, "because they've got energy and some of them are funny. But Ernie would pick my bones. And so would those guys in production. And so would Neil Purkey."

"You seem to have surrounded yourself with cutthroats."

"Ernie's got twin daughters. College money. Put that down. Did you do Emily?"

"I'm running out of paper."

"Big men make enemies. Lincoln. Martin Luther King."

"I guess the difference is, they had supporters."

Harry looked hurt. I felt a little guilty about my remark.

"I will too, someday," he said after a moment. "I see myself, but more importantly I see all the homeless people, working on every conceivable project, not just back in California, but all over. Produced by the homeless. Assembled by the homeless. Built by the homeless. *Second Chances* magazine is the beginning of the end of the primary tragedy of present-day human existence."

"Harry, I know you hate negativity, but a lot of homeless people won't fit into your company. You've got people with mental problems, chemical problems—"

"AA doesn't work for everybody either," said Harry. "But it works for a lot. And that's what *Second Chances* is gonna do. You think I'm an idiot, but I'm not."

"I'm not saying you can't do it—"

"I know I can do it. All I need is start-up capital and breath in my body. Do Neil."

I wrote Neil Purkey's name down. I knew Neil pretty well. He was my best friend for a while at *Who's Hot,* until we got tired of each other's stories. We used to go out drinking now and then, and make each other laugh. Neil still intended to write for television, but most of us thought he'd missed the boat on that one. He was old for a sitcom writer. It's pretty easy to see when somebody else is kidding himself.

Neil and I had once watched one of those financial stories on CNN where they talked about how much you should have put away for retirement at our ages. We hadn't. He wasn't likely to fare any better than me if he lost his job. Even so, I couldn't see him as a killer. I could picture him dancing on Harry's grave but not stuffing him into it.

"These people wouldn't kill anybody," I said. "Not even you."

"Did you put down your ex-girlfriend?"

I gave him the steely glare.

"What's so impossible?" Harry said. "Her and Fairbanks, working together to knock me off. Huh? Or how about you? It could be you. If I could figure how you worked the tuna."

"It's a long flight," I said. "Let's save me for last."

I looked back at my pad, then over at Carole. Harry followed my gaze.

"No," he said flatly. "She could have killed me anytime. I've made myself totally vulnerable to that woman, physically and emotionally. I've told her my dreams and my nightmares."

"What nightmares?"

"Oh, well. Just the one. You know. I told you once."

"The one where your obituary's in the paper? With no photo?"

"Well, yeah, it's the only recurring one."

He looked at her raptly. She was his favorite show. She was sacked out on the five center seats, stretched out on her side—the way *I* like to sleep—with her head toward the far aisle and her boots facing us.

"She looks so . . . so . . . " he said, groping.

"Sinister."

"What the hell are you talking about?"

"Well, she's been present at every one of your accidents. I hope she didn't loosen the gas cap on the jet."

On the last page of the pad, I made a pie chart with the names of the *Who's Hot* people in the sections. I included Neil, Eden, Steve, Jimmy, Peter, Bobbi, Ernie and Emily Hahn. I left Joanne off. I put everyone else in a larger section I called "the field." Then I put it on the seat between Harry and me and began scrunching around, trying to get comfortable. I wasn't optimistic; it's hard to sleep on your side when you're sitting. Harry picked up my pie and stared at it. Then he put it down and closed his eyes.

He was asleep within five minutes. He could sleep sitting; he didn't even have to tilt his seat back.

. . .

We landed at 3 P.M. London time, which was 6 A.M. to me. I was so groggy that when a brisk, brusque woman at the head of the disembarkation line at Heathrow asked me why I'd come to England, I couldn't think of the words "business" or "vacation."

"I thought it would be fun," I said lamely.

"Vacation," she said crisply, and told me to go over that way.

Harry had used the money he saved on our airfare to book us into a prestigious old hotel, the St. Simon's, in Westminster. It was within walking distance of Parliament, Buckingham Palace and New Scotland Yard. Harry wanted to approach John Easter from a suitable base. He also liked the idea of being near Scotland Yard in case something else happened to him. He wanted that machinery handy, working to find his killer.

When we checked in, Carole went up to her room and Harry and I went to our suite, which consisted of two tiny, tastefully furnished compartments. I took the bed near the window overlooking Caxton Street. I lay down on my stomach, starfish style. I didn't even make it to my side. We weren't scheduled to meet Easter until the following afternoon, and a good thing too.

I vaguely recall Harry coming in that night and telling me something about the beggars and buskers in the West End. He'd taken Carole to Covent Garden market. He said the street singers here were better than ours, and something about "opening a London branch." I went back to sleep while he was talking to me.

The next morning, the morning of the ninth, Carole wanted to go to some kind of flea market in the Portobello Road and Harry took her there. We agreed to meet at Trafalgar Square at noon and I went off on my own for a while.

I've read books by veteran Londoners like Dirk Bogarde and Spike Milligan who observe, each in his own way, that the old town has gone pretty thoroughly to hell. And for them, of course, deterioration would be apparent—they knew the city before the

Blitz. But to me, on this day, it was splendid. I felt connected to it.

The man who was the source of the "according to" remarks I've waded through over the years, Edmond Hoyle, lived in London in the 1700s. I'm not truly sure we're related, but Dad always kind of claimed him as a forebear. Edmond Hoyle codified the whist rules. Later he wrote about backgammon and chess. He stymied those players who like to ring in new rules on you as soon as you get ahead. He set the standards. He made an effort to get things right.

In California we tend to erase the past, but London carries it along. You don't have to care about the history, but it's available if you do, in the architecture and in the shops. I saw more anti-quarian bookstores in one little alley, Cecil Court, than I'd ever seen in Orange County.

They even had *our* history. In a cinema memorabilia shop off Charing Cross Road that morning I found some old movie studio flyers—8 x 10 slick publicity mailings sent to U.K. theater owners back when the films came out. One of them was for *The Big Kiss-off,* from 1959, starring Marty Best, one of my Where Did They Go? actors. Marty was not only a Where Did They Go? but a Should Have Been Hot. His career as a star was ruined by unlucky fashion timing. He looked good in a mustache at a time—the mid-to-late fifties—when mustaches were out for leading men. And when Marty shaved his mustache off, he was devoid of appeal. Marty now lived in Huntington Beach and didn't have much mem-orabilia; when I'd interviewed him he'd said his grandchildren didn't know he'd ever done anything. So I picked up the flyer for four pounds. It had a strong drawing of Marty and Dorothy Dean, under the film's English title: *The Butler's Revenge.*

The weather was startlingly fine that day; there was no fog, no rain. It was sunny and uniformly beautiful, with just enough chill to keep you exhilarated. I took a double-decker bus to the Tower of London and back to the West End, where I got off at

Trafalgar Square to meet Harry and Carole. They were standing in front of Nelson's column, along with several hundred pigeons.

"We just got here; we took the tube," said Carole cheerily, holding up two bags of stuff she'd bought at the market. She looked up at the monument. "I was in this square with Dad; I remember, I sat on one of the lions."

The meeting with Easter was to take place at three o'clock. Harry had originally planned a pre-meeting nap for himself, but he was so pleased by Carole's obvious good spirits that when she expressed an interest in seeing Buckingham Palace, he agreed instantly. We tubed back to the hotel to drop off Carole's bags and then trooped over to the palace gates, where we joined a crowd of tourists and natives staring across the paved yard at a pair of red-uniformed guards who marched back and forth at intervals.

"Like they could hold off all of us," said Carole.

"How about this?" suggested Harry. "A walk in the park, lunch in a pub, a little prep for the meeting. You guys be Easter, and I'll be me."

St. James's Park stretches from the palace toward Parliament Square. There's a long lake in it, and Harry had me take a picture of him and Carole at the foot of this lake, under a weeping willow tree, with the fairy-tale vista of Whitehall architecture behind them. Then we strolled beside the water, toward Whitehall, keeping pace with the royal waterfowl. There were trees and rolling lawn to our right.

I was feeling odd and peaceful, at home somehow. I was walking where illustrious Englishmen had walked—Hoyle; Hitchcock; Halliwell, the great film historian. I was open to all kinds of vagrant thoughts. I felt part of the continuity, like a bead on a string. I felt I was on the verge of figuring something out about myself.

"This is the only city I've ever been in that's been bombed," I said. I looked back at the section of park through which we'd come, and walked backward for a moment.

Harry said, "That's what Joe likes to do. He walks forward but he looks backward. Good way to fall on your ass."

"Who is that back there?" I wondered. "He's been hopping from tree to tree behind us and now he's waving."

Harry stopped and peered back at the trees. Behind a venerable willow some fifty yards away was a man in an off-white trench coat, gesticulating. He shocked us all by calling, "Harry! Harry!"

"He *knows* me," Harry murmured, squinting and starting toward the tree.

"Wait a minute," I said.

In my new capacity as sidekick, I moved forward and to the side, circling across the sun-dappled grass to get a better look at the guy who was waving at us. Carole walked behind me.

"Is it that guy from production?" she asked.

"Who, Steve? I don't think so. Hey! Steve?"

"No, no," said the guy genially. "It's me. Art."

TWELVE

We approached Art Klee carefully. As we did so I recalled reading that he was supposed to be working on a picture in the U.K., which explained his presence in England. But it didn't quite account for his presence under a weeping willow tree in St. James's Park. He gestured for the three of us to join him under its overhanging branches.

"C'mon, c'mon," he encouraged us. "We can play again."

Harry stepped through the curtain of drooping leaves; Carole and I followed, moving off to his left as Harry and Klee faced each other under the willow's canopy.

"It's tough to bring a gun into England on a plane," he explained as we approached, "but we're doing this picture here—the fiftieth version of *Robin Hood*; it's actually called that—and I bribed the prop guy to let me take this off the location."

From under his trench coat he produced a crossbow. It had an arrow fitted into the notch, or slot.

"I gotta bring it back," Art continued, "or at least I gotta bring the bow back. I don't think he cares so much about the arrows. See? I've got some more arrows here, on this belt quiver. They call 'em quarrels. We can do just like at the paintball field. Oh, wait.

I forgot to bring a bow for you." He gave Harry an apologetic "Oops" look.

Art looked different. He had a full beard, apparently for the role he was playing, and the hair on his head was darker, and thicker. Like many actors, and unlike humans, his hairline was growing lower as he aged. He was in excellent humor, to judge from his expression. The only wider smile I'd ever seen was on The Joker.

"Can't believe my luck finding you here," he said.

"You mean you were just walking around St. James's Park with a crossbow?" I asked.

"Well," said Art, and shrugged. "Actually, I found out you were here. I called your office. The tough part was finding out where you were staying. Your secretary didn't know. But she knew who you were seeing here, and turned out, John Easter's office knew where you were. Then all I had to do was camp out. I saw you come out of your hotel a little while ago. I been following you." He looked around to make sure no one else was approaching and grinned. "This is gonna be great."

"Hey, Art, you better not wave that around," I said, indicating the crossbow. "That's an ugly-lookin' thing there. You could trans-fix somebody with that. I'll bet they've got a lot of bobbies and guards around here too."

"Well, I got a permit. I mean, *we* do, on the picture, to have these here," Art said. "At the worst, I'm overrehearsing. So as long as we're inconspicuous . . ."

"I'm not sure you can shoot that thing inconspicuously, Art," said Harry.

"Let's find out," said Klee.

"I take it you saw our most recent issue."

"Well, let me think." Art leaned against the tree, holding the crossbow with the arrow pointing down. He craned his neck around the tree trunk at the strollers on the walkway. They were couples mostly, some with baby carriages or toddlers. There were a few picnickers in the grass farther on toward Whitehall. The traffic on the street just off the park went by. We didn't have any-one's attention, and we were largely concealed by the willow branches anyway.

"Was that the one with the lists in it?" mused Art. "Because I did see that one. Is that the last one? The one where you said of all the people in the universe, there'd be nine great wastes of time in the next century? One of whom is me? I saw that one."

His smile had become a little garish. But Harry showed no uneasiness. He didn't even stare at the crossbow, which I was doing most of the time.

"I just had a thought about a meeting I've got coming up," said Harry. "Can I reach in my pocket? I want to write a note to myself. I'll show it to you when I'm done."

"Sure," said Klee, with some curiosity.

Harry produced his memo pen and a small notebook and poised the pen over the paper.

"You know," he said, resonantly, "you should listen to Joe here. I think there are rules against shooting that crossbow, even if you're Art Klee."

"That's a memo pen, isn't it?" said Klee. "I keep up with new stuff like that. I love a nice gadget. Toss it over."

Harry complied. Klee caught the pen left-handed and talked into it himself.

"You know what I hate?" he told the pen, chattily. He was very hyper, very on. "If I had a magazine, and I could make my list of people least necessary, I'd put at the top . . . people who don't appreciate how hard comedy is. Now, you say you've got a sense of humor, but nobody ever gets to test you. See, you're al-ways grading me; I never get to grade you. And you can wreck me, but I'm not allowed to wreck you. It's hard to be funny," he went on, putting the pen in his trench coat pocket and peering around the tree trunk again. "And just to prove my point . . . I thought what we'd do . . . I thought we'd see if you could be funny.

Under pressure. Because that's how I have to do it. A lot of times it's easier at, say, a party, to be funny, than it is on a set, or on location, with a crew standing around. Everybody's bored. Maybe you don't have any good lines? That's a tough one. There's only so many situations. There's only so many good writers. Sometimes the material just isn't there. So you gotta come up with something, do your rope tricks so it's entertaining. You really sweat it out. You really worry about it. And then when it comes out, here's some leaky dick who tells you We're Not Amused. Well, that's fair enough. But he doesn't stop there. He doesn't just say, 'This guy's last picture wasn't funny.' He says to the industry, 'Don't hire this guy. Let him starve.' It's not journalism. It's assault. Ever been assaulted?"

"Little bit lately," said Harry mildly. He glanced at the cross-bow as Art raised it slightly.

"So now my agent is saying it's kind of tough to find a fat part anymore. No more leads, and those strong character parts, you know, they always go to one guy, whoever's the character man of the month. Used to be Jack Warden got 'em all, then it was John Mahoney. Now it's this punk Fleger all of a sudden who's hot. I got him the breakthrough part.

"Anyway," said Art earnestly, "I'm so tired of telling you don't do this, and then you go ahead and do it. So we got a new arrangement. Since you're incorrigible. I'm gonna shoot you. There's only one thing that can stop me from shooting you. And that's if you can be funny in this situation. We'll see how you do."

Carole Spangler gave Klee a look of combined surprise and distaste.

"Guy can't take criticism?" she muttered to me.

"It's a personal thing he's got with Harry," I muttered back.

"Oh," said Carole, and nodded. She seemed to get that all right.

Harry was looking from the crossbow to Art Klee with his head cocked to one side.

"This is 'Be funny or I'll kill you'?" he asked.

"More less," said Klee.

Harry nodded, thinking it over.

"You don't have all the time in the world either," said Klee. "In my business, when we're on, we're on. I used to work live every week, y'know."

"You were good then," said Harry. I never would have had the nerve to say that. I thought it was reckless, even for Harry. I was flicking my eyeballs around, trying to see someone official who could break this tableau up, but I couldn't spot anyone.

"Do I have to use my own material?" asked Harry.

Klee considered for a moment.

"I don't want to be unfair," he said finally. "I usually use somebody else's. But that's not really an advantage. I should make you say, 'Fie on thee, for thou art my foe and I defy thee. I da-fee, da-fie, da-foe thee.' That's one of my lines in this one. But I want to give you a chance."

"Okay," said Harry. "How do we score this? Do you have to laugh, or is it good enough if you intellectually understand that it's funny?"

Klee turned cold. He leveled the crossbow at Harry, from the hip.

"You're on," he said.

I was imagining what it must be like to have an arrow enter at the belly, and it made me feel anything but humorous. Besides which, in my own past, whenever anyone, like a woman or a little kid, had demanded that I say something funny, I had always immediately dried up and blanked. And that was without the crossbow. Harry had the absolute toughest audience a comic could have.

But when you caught Harry Poe in this kind of spot, you caught him at his best. He loved a challenge. And in this particular instance, he was being asked to perform in front of Carole Spangler. So his mighty brain was operating at full wattage. He straightened up, rubbed his hands and addressed Klee without a tremor.

"Okay," he said. "I read this in the Mr. Boffo comic strip in the *L.A. Times*. This guy Boffo is an Everyman type, a loser who gets in all these situations. So in this one, he's out in the backyard barbecuing, he's got his chef's hat and his apron, but there's a storm, a sudden rain, and it's just ruined his barbecue. So he's so enraged, he grabs a garden hose and he sprays it straight up at the sky, and he's screaming out, 'All right, two can play at that game!' "

Harry acted it out as he did it, and although his delivery was not professional and he misquoted slightly—I've since seen the joke in a Mr. Boffo compendium and it's funnier on paper—he preserved the point of the joke, and even got a snort of surprise out of Carole Spangler, which, under the circumstances, counts as a laugh.

Art Klee frowned. He was in a quandary. He'd expected Harry to gag—not to come *up* with a gag. Now he had a borderline situation to deal with. Harry was waiting, his eyes and conscience clear, prepared to live or die with that joke.

The sun shone on the lawns of St. James's Park, and under an ancient tree, one yeoman, crossbow in hand, faced an unarmed man.

Klee's face darkened.

I thought I should do something. Harry had asked me to be his sidekick. Implicit in the request was that I should stick up for him, for the week, at least. But I didn't feel like jumping in front of him and taking an arrow.

Carole and I were off to Klee's right side a bit, and he had largely lost interest in us. It occurred to me to surreptitiously reach into Carole Spangler's leather bag.

"Long as we're using props, Art," I said, coming out of it with the Facer, "you might be interested in this. You probably don't know what it is. . . ."

My thinking, as I look back on it, seems to have been that I might get Klee to drop his weapon by intimidating him with the Facer. It wasn't until I hefted it and showed it to him that I realized how faux it looked. And when Klee turned the crossbow toward me, I found that the phase of fearlessness and unconcern for my own personal safety that had begun when Joanne left me had finally topped out, and ended. I couldn't take my eyes off the arrowhead. I didn't miss Joanne at that moment; my last thought would not have been of her. It would just have been an indiscriminate Oh God.

But to my astonishment, Klee didn't sneer at the sight of the Facer. He blanched and backed into the tree.

"Know what it is?" he repeated. "I *invested* in it. That's the fucking Facer. Don't point that thing at me, I saw a demonstration. How'd you get that in the country? Those are outlawed." He lowered the crossbow. "Put it down, I'm not kiddin'. That beam'll go through me, the tree, the palace and the goddamn royal family. Put it down."

I pointed it off to the side.

"Where did that come from?" Klee wanted to know.

"My husband invented it," said Carole.

"Kevin Face is your husband?"

"Was."

"Well, that bastard cost me some change, and he should be stopped, wherever he is. If he's still making those, he should be banned. That's a person who BELONGS on your twenty-first-century shit list."

"All right, then, drop the bow," I said. There was a pause. Klee eyeballed the Facer. Then he took a deep breath and leaned his crossbow, arrowhead down, against the tree trunk.

"I've been unhappy," he said.

He sank to a sitting position against the tree as Harry walked up to him.

"Performers are creatures of emotion," Harry said. "I'd like my pen back."

Klee dug it out and handed it up to him. Then he sighed. He seemed to have to go way down for each breath. His head went back against the tree trunk.

"I know I was bad in *Smoker's Cough,*" he said matter-of-factly. "I couldn't find the laughs. I was like some old guy I used to make fun of." He sighed again, and looked up into the branches. "Now look at me. Da-fee, da-fie, da-foe." His eyes misted.

Harry was perplexed. He looked from Carole to me as if to ask what he was expected to do.

"I don't know what to tell you, Art," he said finally. "You were gonna kill me just now."

"No I wasn't," said Klee, rubbing his eyelids gently. "It doesn't even work. Look, the trigger doesn't catch. The bolt just sits there in the groove. I couldn't take a working crossbow around London. I wanted to humiliate you. I thought you'd pee in your pants."

We all took this in. Art and I had faced each other with handfuls of nothing.

"Well, in that case . . . ," Harry said finally, and squatted beside Klee. "In that case, I got one word for you. Are you ready? Drama."

Klee looked at his feet, stretched out before him, and said nothing.

"You were very convincing just now," Harry went on quietly. "And it was easy, wasn't it? You know it was. Drama's easier. And you get more respect anyway. Everybody does it when they get older. Robin Williams does it. Jack Lemmon did it. Fuckin' Jerry Lewis did it. It's no shame."

He took off his glasses and wiped them on the hem of Klee's trench coat.

"Make the switch, Art. Make it soon. You'll do well. 'Cause you are turning into a real Zagnut bar."

We left him there, sitting against the willow tree.

. . .

The new plan was for us to walk Carole back to the hotel and
then go on to the meeting with John Easter, which was now just
an hour away. But as we walked down Caxton Street the plan
changed again.

Carole had been meandering along thoughtfully, slowing us
up, casting glances at Harry from time to time. Now she reached
a decision and picked up the pace.

"Okay," she said, looking at him. "Let's go."

"Whaddya mean?" he asked. "We're going."

"I mean let's go," she said, distinctly. Harry stared at her un-
comprehendingly as we kept walking. She stopped finally, and we
did too. "You and me. My room. Let's do the locomotion."

Harry was struck dumb.

"What, you . . . want to have sex?" he asked.

She looked exasperated.

"Only if you're up to it," she said. "Yeah, I thought we should
try it. That whole scene back there was, I don't know, you were
good in that situation, it was impressive. . . . I guess it got my juices
flowing. And you've been staring at me since the cave. It's time we
just . . . Come on," she finished peremptorily, and walked on toward the hotel. "Come on."

Harry and I followed along, more slowly. This sudden intro-
duction of the earthy note in Carole's attitude was what he'd been
hoping for, but it was unexpected. Abrupt. Harry looked as though
his dreams might have come truer than he was ready for. He
seemed considerably more disconcerted than he had facing Art
Klee's crossbow. I sympathized.

"Hope you're in the zone," I said.

"Jesus," he muttered.

"Just remember: This is what you've been waiting for. Your
whole life has been leading up to this. On-ramp to on-ramp."

"Shut up."

Carole turned at the main entrance to face us.

"Are you coming?" she demanded. In her tight jeans and turtleneck, she looked tough.

Harry squinted, as if into the sun.

"That first one is always iffy," he murmured.

I nodded. "Sometimes it's so iffy it's the last one."

Harry walked slowly away from me, up the steps, and met Carole at the door. Then he followed her into the lobby.

"Don't forget you got a meeting," I called after him.

THIRTEEN

I sat on a little hallway couch on the 12th floor of the Easter Building—Easter Island, they call it—in the Strand. The building formerly housed a gentlemen's club, but John Easter bought it in the eighties and now it was his home and headquarters in the city. The 12th was the top floor. I'd come up in an old elevator that smelled like cigars, with an operator who sat on a stool. On the 12th floor I was met by a security guard, who walked me down a narrow, carpeted hallway. He sat me down facing a receptionist whose desk was along the opposite wall, outside a big brown mahogany door.

Her name was Noelle, she had a fresh, round face and she was from Trinidad-Tobago. Well, Tobago. She was very nice. I got to know her pretty well because I sat on the dark green couch across from her for twenty minutes, waiting for Harry.

Noelle phoned into Easter's office to say that Mr. Hoyle was here for the three o'clock, but Mr. Poe wasn't yet. She listened for a moment, then hung up and told me to make myself comfortable on the couch. I didn't really feel that awkward. We were late, but I was on time. Besides, I had nothing at stake. If Easter fumed and seethed behind the big brown door because Harry was tardy, it was no skin off me. In any battle of the magnates, they'd be shooting way over my head.

I tried to keep Noelle talking because her accent was so elegant and she had a unique turn of phrase. She said she'd been in London for two years, and that Easter was a passable boss.

"It's a good job," she said. "Sometimes the hours are long. That's the only fly in my perfect world of ointment."

I asked whether John Easter might be getting mad in there.

"I don't know," she said, glancing toward the door. "I haven't seen him yet today."

I figured if Harry didn't show up by 3:30 I'd slide on out of the building. At 3:20 he came out of the elevator.

He wore his charcoal gray suit with a navy blue tie. The look on his face matched the sobriety of his attire. His face was angular behind his glasses.

I didn't know if I should ask how it had gone or not. The phrase "How's your tip?" jumped to mind, but I squelched it; he didn't look as he had the night he'd introduced us all to Yasmine. So I just asked if he was ready.

"Oh, yeah," he said, and nodded to Noelle.

"How's everything?" I asked.

He bobbed his head up and down, with a kind of hyper-preoccupied air. Noelle buzzed Easter and then sent us through the brown door.

We entered a big living room/studio, cluttered with food cartons and magazines, clothes and guitars, keyboards, synthesizers, cables, microphones with stands, a drum kit, a big-screen TV, couches, pillows, little tables, folding chairs. The windows which looked out on the Strand were closed, so the air was stale.

Easter sat on the biggest couch, a great brown leather thing in the middle of the room. He motioned us to matching chairs facing it.

I'd expected a piercing glance and a ruthless demeanor from John Easter, but he had a kind of dissipated air about him. He looked about 40, a little paunchy, with blue, kind of buggy eyes; they were bleary this afternoon. He wore a big Hawaiian shirt over shorts. His fingers were startling: His left hand was neatly manicured, but the fingernails on his right hand were long and yellow. He was kind of a half Howard Hughes.

He saw me staring and said, "Guitar. I pick with this hand and of course, chords with the other."

"Ah," I said.

"Frustrated rocker," he said. "Had to settle for billions."

He offered us eye-openers—gin and tonic. Harry said sure. Easter leaned forward and pressed a button on a console on the coffee table. "Two, George," he said.

Easter rubbed his eyes while looking at me. He slouched on the couch and sighed.

"I'm outnumbered," he observed.

"Joe's my conscience," said Harry. "He'll keep me from trying to cheat you. Also he's my memory. You should see him at the office. He knows every movie; remembers the cast of everything."

Easter cocked his head at me, with mild interest. He blinked slowly while George, a young black man in a mess jacket, came in with the drinks. Easter took a sip of his gin and tonic and shuddered, grimacing and half-sneezing like young Danny Kaye.

"The key," he explained, "is the first swallow. If you don't bring it right back up, it's smooth sailing." He looked at me.

"Name the actors who played the Magnificent Seven," he said.

"Brad Dexter," I began, to save time. Easter raised a hand in acknowledgment. He took a healthy swallow of his gin, this time with only a slight shiver. "I love the Westerns," he said. "They release my sentiment. I sore an old *Rifleman* last time I was in the States. I'd seen it before; I anticipated every scene and most of the dialogue. Came the end, music up . . . little Johnny Crawford runs to his pa . . . I wept like an old woman. That's what people don't understand about people like us, Harry. We're just a couple of softies. That's why we love the films. My family didn't get telly until I was four. Night we got it, Dad set it up in the parlor. Masked men robbed the stage. I flinched when they shot their guns at the camera. Had to sit on Mum's lap or I couldn't watch. But I had to watch, didn't I? I've got big eyes today because they stuck wide, watching your cowboys." He surveyed his fingernails and looked around distractedly. "Do you like music? I had some people in here last night . . . we did a song I wrote myself and it sounded quite good, but I hesitate to play it now."

We insisted, of course. Easter got up and made his way, like John Wayne through the steers in *Red River,* through the folding chairs, amps and instruments to the recording equipment in the corner. He messed with that for a few moments and then played us a take of three guitars, drums and keyboard—something instrumental in the style of Peter Townshend. In fact, I might go so far as to say it was appropriated. It sounded a lot like "Won't Get Fooled Again," but a vocal started after about two minutes and this version had different lyrics.

We listened dutifully until it was finished. It took eight or ten minutes, the way songs will when you're playing informally. Easter walked around the room, listening. George came in during the song with two more drinks. Harry and Easter accepted their refills. When the song finally ended, Harry said it had sounded good, which it had. Stolen, but good.

"Y'know, I think it did," agreed Easter. He took a sip. "I stopped drinking once, for a year. Didn't play a note. Lost the inclination. Had to start up drinking again, in moderation; couldn't sacrifice me music. Either of you lads play an instrument?"

Harry and I looked at each other, doubtfully. Everyone in our generation had intended to make the cover of *Rolling Stone* at one moment or another. We'd all learned the chords. But there was a reason we'd all gone into other fields.

"We messed around in school," said Harry. "I played a little drums. Joe here—"

"I had four years of piano when I was a kid," I said. "All I can play now is the theme from *Exodus*."

"Well, you know chords, surely," said Easter, picking up a guitar. "I'm not really in shape for anything hard. I thought something more introspective this early. Here's one I've been working on."

He sat on a stool, setting his drink down beside him, and gave us something unplugged—the theme from *The Deer Hunter,* only slower.

"Is that yours?" I asked. Harry shot me a dirty look.

Easter looked up.

"No, actually it's *The Deer Hunter*."

"Nice," said Harry.

"Isn't it?" said Easter, negotiating his way through a tricky section with great care.

I made my way over to an old keyboard setup—an old electric piano, rather than a synthesizer. Harry went over and sat at Easter's drum kit, a little baffled. There's not much you can do on drums with the theme from *The Deer Hunter*.

Easter held his final note until it faded away. He put the acoustic guitar down, took a sip of his drink and picked up a Les Paul electric. He also brought up *Who's Hot* for the first time.

"It's crisp," he said, plugging himself in. "I love that break at the middle. Hot and Not. Winners and losers. It's harsh, but it provides the opportunity for that great leap over the staples from right to left, back to front, from down and out to up on top. Quintessentially American. Who's Hot. Slash. Who's Not." He took another sip. "Having said which, I could bring out my own magazine and call it *Up and Down*."

Harry shrugged. "Others have tried it," he said. "People tend to come back to the real thing."

Easter smiled and made a small, slow, graceful arc of dismissal with his right hand, the one with the fingernails.

"If I don't like what I intend to buy, I'm a fool. I think I could tolerate a beat now. Something simple. 'Birthday'?"

He meant the Beatles song, of course. He seemed to center around 1969 musically. Hesitantly at first and then with more authority, Harry laid down a basic British rock intro, heavy on beats one and three. Easter played the bass line from "Birthday." I put in some treble chords. It was hideous. You wouldn't think you could screw up a song as elementary as "Birthday," but Harry and I hadn't played in some years.

Easter seemed pleased, however; I don't think he'd expected much. Our version of "Birthday" was about fifteen minutes long. After it, we each played incompatible fragments for a few moments. Easter leaned down to pick up his drink, took a sip and put it back on the floor.

"Let's pretend I've already said this is as high as I can go, and you've said this is as low as you accept. So for the entire plant— TV and print—where does that put us?"

"It puts me at thirty million."

Easter picked his drink up again.

"My original offer was fair."

"I have a lot of incentive to hold on to *Who's Hot*. It's my baby. I've got a lot of fine people there."

There was a little glow in Easter's eyes. He grinned boyishly.

"I hear one of them's trying to kill you," he said.

Harry must have been as surprised as I was, but he didn't flinch. He barked a laugh.

"Who told you that?"

"Wesley."

"Who told Wesley?"

"Wesley's reliable."

"I know Wesley." Harry showed a trace of irritation. "I had a small run-in with an irate employee. It's not a problem."

"Which irate employee?"

A good question. Harry bypassed it.

"I'll handle it, John. The issue will be completely resolved before you move in."

"During negotiations for my purchase of the *London Tribune*," Easter said reminiscently, "one of the employees—he drove a truck, you'd say, in the circulation department—threatened the owner, in the city room. And when I became the owner, I inherited the threats." He looked sadly at Harry. "This man managed, somehow, to get into my office, while I wasn't there. He was even able to get up here. And leave me notes. He hid, an entire night, in a cupboard in my bedroom. You may not be afraid of your man, but perhaps you should be. It's not that hard for a lunatic to kill someone. They do it every day." He looked around, recalling his ordeal.

"What finally happened?"

"I was extremely fortunate." His eyebrows rose in reminiscent surprise. "He died. I think he died of hate, actually. He was consumed, from inside." He rubbed his chest. "Heart attack." He regarded Harry mildly. "You say your situation would be resolved before I moved in. But it needs to be resolved before the deal is done. I can't go in myself, or send anyone else in, while there's someone running around the shop acting the fool."

Harry looked a bit stymied for a moment.

"All right," he said finally, "how about this? Assuming we root out this thorn in my paw, what are you willing to pay for the whole show. Ballpark."

"I might move in the direction of your figure," said Easter, sipping his drink and rising. "What do you say we play it back?" He moved toward his recording equipment.

I cleared my throat and mouthed the word "staff" at Harry. He looked back at me, uncomprehending.

"Staff," I said.

"What?" asked Harry.

"Staff," I said loudly.

"Oh, yeah." Harry turned to Easter. "Joe wanted me to put

in a condition on the sale, that you either keep the staff predominantly intact or you offer them a severance package equivalent to the one I offer."

Easter cast me a glance.

"This isn't a union shop, is it?"

"No," I said, "but Harry's always maintained benefits consistent with Guild scale."

"Right. Well," said Easter, "Harry of course has his people and I mine. I certainly couldn't accept any restrictions on whom to employ."

"It's Harry's people," I said, "who have made the magazine attractive enough for you to want."

"And it's my people," he replied cheerily, "who have contributed to my success in every fookin' thing I've ever done." He gazed at me with polite exasperation. "You know, I'm beginning to wonder if this band is ever going to tour."

Easter went over to his tape console. Harry leaned over at the drums to hiss at me.

"I think it would behoove you," Harry told me, "to play a few bars of 'The Rifleman.' "

To my dismay, Easter had recorded our trio playing "Birthday," and now, having rewound, he treated us to some of it. It was ghastly, although now and then you'd hear a few decent bars.

"Needs a vocal," Easter murmured. He clicked it off and turned to me.

"No doubt I'll love the present staff if they're all as charming as you," he said. "But rumor has it that one of them is otherwise."

"We can discuss staff when we're further on," said Harry.

"I think that's reasonable," said Easter.

He told us he had to talk to some people from the City—the financial section of London—who were waiting for him. So Harry dropped his sticks and we departed. Easter's last words were, "Remember: No mad old retainers hiding below stairs."

Harry didn't speak in the elevator on the way down. He didn't speak until we got out onto the Strand and began walking toward Charing Cross Station. Then he said, "I think it went all right."

"Whaddya mean? He knows about your accidents and he won't buy unless you find out who's doing it."

"I meant with Carole."

We walked on.

"Oh," I said finally.

"In fact, considering how it could have gone, it went great. It wasn't the best I've ever done, but the important thing is, we did it."

"Well, good."

"The balance has shifted. I've established my beachhead. She can't push me back into the sea."

"Well . . . ," I said, at something of a loss. "On to Berlin."

"What I wish is that we'd had time to go ahead and do it again. You know. Kind of . . ." He cleared his throat.

"Underline it?"

"Build on it," he said coldly. "I had to leave to get dressed. We were in her room. She fell asleep."

I nodded.

"Worn out, huh?"

Harry looked at me irritably.

"Yeah, Joe. I exhausted her."

He walked off the curb and nearly got hit by a truck coming around the corner from the right. I pulled him back.

"You should cross with the natives," I told him.

Harry looked up and down the street, suddenly cheerful and resolute. His eyes had cleared.

"I'll take her shopping," he said.

•   •   •

That night we three ate dinner in the hotel restaurant, an ornate banquet room frequented by MPs who stayed at the St. Simon's because of its proximity to Parliament. Carole wore a calf-length black dress which Harry had bought her at Harrods an hour before. He called it a tea dress and she called it an LBD—Little Black Dress. She looked good in it too; slim and tanned from her outdoor lifestyle.

She seemed distracted and unsure of herself. At first I thought it might be because of the surroundings, which were pretty haute. But she fit the room all right; there was nothing coarse about her this evening. She pronounced the French dishes correctly for the waiter—something the English don't always care to do.

Still, she was oddly subdued. The dishes she pronounced so correctly were vetoed by Harry as soon as she spoke. He ordered for her. He was proprietary. She took it. I couldn't really figure it out. She wasn't submitting playfully, as part of a new kind of kidding, ardent, lovers' relationship. She didn't seem to like what he was doing, but she didn't say anything back. She'd lost her aggressiveness. She looked worried, uneasy—like people do when they think they might've left the gas on back at the house.

The waiter mentioned wine, but Harry vetoed that too.

"Don't get us started," he said merrily.

Harry was oblivious to any undercurrent of distress at the table. He looked forward to our return to L.A. the next day. He spoke of Art Klee, and some other actors he knew, and advanced the theory that American comic performers stop being funny at age fifty. I mentioned George Burns, and Harry said grandly, "Well, a hundred, then." Then he started talking about *Second Chances*.

"What makes you think Easter's gonna buy *Who's Hot*?" I interrupted. "You don't know who's been giving you the hotfoot over at the office. How are you gonna find out? All Easter said today was no."

"The key," he explained, "is to take the deal-breaking obstacle and make it part of the plan."

He asked what I intended to do for work when we got back to L.A.

"I don't know," I said. "I thought I'd wait till after the holidays before I start to sweat."

He shook his head.

"You shouldn't've quit me," he said. "You lost your venue. What are you gonna do without me? When it's all over, and you're on your deathbed, looking back, what are you going to say to justify yourself? What are you gonna put up as your great achievement in life?"

"I guess I'll say, 'I worked for Harry Poe longer than anybody else did.' "

He even laughed at that. He was in a great mood. He picked out a dessert for Carole too, but she said she didn't feel well and excused herself.

"But we're going out," said Harry as she stood up.

"I don't think I'm up to it," she said.

"Whaddya mean, you look great. Come on, it's our last night here."

"It's been a busy day." She stood there smoothing her dress, looking at the table.

"Well, *that's* true enough," he allowed. "Okay. Okay. Get some rest and I'll pound on your door tomorrow. We've got to get up early."

She nodded. As she walked away, Harry said to me, "That dress really works. When we get back I'm going to get her a whole wardrobe. No reason she shouldn't look that good all the time."

FOURTEEN

Looking back now, I can see that all three of us had made, or were making, resolutions by the time we flew home. On the most superficial level, I was determined to beat Carole to those five seats in the middle, but this time, of course, they were occupied, so the three of us sat together, with Harry at the window and Carole in between.

Harry had clearly reached some decision about *Who's Hot*; he was making cheerful comments about how he'd run the airline, the kind of thing he does when he's normal. He lived for the kind of situation Easter had presented him with, where he had to beat somebody.

"We're gonna bust that logjam," he assured me.

He was full of plans for *Second Chances*.

"We'll get some office space and do some dummy issues first, make sure we got the right team. You're on at twice your old salary if you want. I love this guy," he told Carole. "He was gonna take an arrow for me."

I made no comment. I needed a job, and before long I'd need one worse. But I had made up my mind not to work for Harry anymore. A foolish decision, probably, but I knew I couldn't return to him permanently. I couldn't go back to someone who had such a low opinion of Where Did They Go.

Harry wore his evangelical look as he went on about *Second Chances*.

"I swear, Joe, this is what I was saved for. This, and you." He said this last to Carole. Then, to my surprise, he started tickling her, overcoming her attempts to slap his hands away. "You're gonna be the first cover. Cover girl, cover girl."

"*Please,*" said Carole.

He finally let up on her, and after our meal he went to sleep, leaving Carole and me to sit through some turbulence together.

Finally I broke the silence. It occurred to me that I'd never heard her express an opinion about *Second Chances,* so I asked her what she thought of the idea.

"I don't know," she said. "It sounds like one of those good-news newspapers they're always talking about."

An intelligent criticism, I thought. She had put her finger on a possible flaw I'd noticed myself—no Not section.

"Have you told him that?" I asked.

"Yeah."

"What did he say?"

"I don't think he heard me."

She held a notebook in her lap with the royal family on the cover. As on the night before, she seemed to be sitting on something she couldn't quite hatch. She turned her movie screen on and got the most recent Schwarzenegger picture. She stared at it for a few moments and then clicked it off.

"Siskel and Ebert liked it," I said.

"Yeah, but your ex-girlfriend and Bobbi LaMott gave it two thumbs down up at the reception desk."

"Then it's probably flawed," I conceded. "They're pretty good on movies."

"Yeah. . . ."

I began reading my copy of volume one of Spike Milligan's

WWII memoirs, *Adolf Hitler: My Part in His Downfall*. I had just gotten to the part where Spike's father was thrown out of the War Ministry ("Father left. With head held high and feet held higher") when Carole turned to me with a look of such urgency that I almost dropped the book.

"Did you ever wake up and say to yourself, I've been living my life all wrong?"

Her brown eyes drilled anxiously into mine. I was taken aback, both by the question and the intensity she brought with it.

"Well . . . ," I said, nodding thoughtfully, "yeah. In fact I woke up to that very thought yesterday in the park, with that Facer in my hand."

"Well, I did too." She threw her head back on the headrest and looked up at the seat belt light. "I woke up yesterday too."

It was clear something serious was coming my way, and for some reason she wanted to confide in me rather than Harry. That meant she probably wanted to confide in me *about* Harry, so I glanced over at him. It wasn't really necessary, though. Harry snored on occasion, and the kind of snore he had—well, you couldn't fake it. He was snoring that way now, his head against the window frame. He was out.

"I told you about my dad," said Carole.

"Yeah. He was a dentist."

"He was a *great* dentist. Stars would ask his advice, not just about their teeth, but about other things. How to face the camera. How they looked best. I'd be in there sometimes and I heard. They *relied* on him. Because he was trustworthy. And he was to me too. He came to every play, he came to my tennis matches. Whenever he said 'I promise,' he did it."

I nodded.

"Well. . . . My mom was an actress. Real attractive, but she lost parts to name actresses. I don't think she was really that close to getting the parts, but she thought she just missed. She got frustrated, and she took it out on Dad. It was like the marriage wasn't what she wanted. She could be bitchy about it. And I think she cheated on him. I admired my dad, but I grew up like Mom. I picked up the bitchy part. Maybe you noticed."

"Not me."

"Anyway. . . ." She took a deep breath. "One day—car crash. They just disappeared. I never saw them, even at the funeral. I wasn't ready. And ever since . . . I've been all over the place. One mistake after another, only it's like the same mistake every time. I keep doing like Mom. I wasn't going to do it with him." She tilted her head toward Harry. "I thought I was okay with him because he was such a jerk, you know? I was detached? But then he was brave in the park, talking into his pen and telling jokes, and I thought, Well, that's impressive. And here the guy's paying my way, and he's brave and everything. . . . Maybe I was looking for Daddy, I don't know. But now he thinks he can tickle me. Did you see that?"

"That was a liberty," I agreed.

"He was in my room this morning telling me what to wear. If I say something, it's like I didn't say anything. When I used to tell him I hated him, he'd just *nod*. Today I said it's not gonna work. He said, Sure it will. I said, No, I'll pay you back for the trip and the room and board, but it's not gonna work. He said, Sure it will. He's got us all mixed up with Carpool Companions and *Second Chances* and magazine covers. . . . He doesn't hear 'No.' And you know what? It's my own fault. That's my big revelation. I bring my bad situations on myself. I choose my company."

She threw her head back on the headrest again.

"Blah blah blah," she said.

"It's okay."

"I had to get it out and it was either you or the flight attendant."

I was silent for a while. Then curiosity overcame me.

"So, yesterday with Harry, uh . . ." I stopped, discreetly.

"I have no one to blame but myself."

She sat with her eyes closed for some time. Then she punched the Schwarzenegger movie back on. After a minute or so she punched it off and began to write rapidly in her notebook. Finally she put the notebook away and fell asleep, along with everyone else in the plane but me and a couple of babies.

• • •

Whenever I go on a trip I get homesick—by which I mean that by the time I get home, I'm sick. It's usually a virus which takes to my chest until it feels like leaving. I knew on the flight that I was in for a good one, and by the time we got back to Laguna, I was floored.

I had just strength enough to holler at Reuben. When we arrived back at the castle, I found Sashi and Savage in Harry's kitchen, unattended, sharing a stick of butter they'd managed to get off the counter and onto the floor. Now, I always figured it was okay for me to eat poorly if I chose to, but Sashi couldn't weigh taste against consequences. She needed someone to oversee her meals. Besides which, I'd pictured how happy she'd be to see me, and instead we started right out arguing over a spot of grease on the floor. It was an emotional letdown.

I found Reuben in the small glass-walled office off the main dining area which he used as Carpool Companion headquarters. He was sitting at one of Harry's computers, typing. His hair was wisped up at the side, as if he'd been running his fingers through it in creative agonies. He didn't look up when I came in.

"Goddamn it, Reuben, who's watching the dogs?"

"Everybody."

"That means nobody."

Harry and Carole had been bringing bags in and dropping them. Harry now came over to join us.

"Hey, who's taking care of the dogs?" he asked indignantly. "They're eating butter in the kitchen."

Reuben shot himself back on his chair wheels and glared up at us.

"I'm trying to write something here," he said. "They've been fine. If they got butter they just now got it. Maybe you'd rather sit in here and be dispatcher and take static from all these tramps."

"What are you writing?" asked Harry, moving toward the screen.

Reuben vaulted forward from his chair and closed it out.

"Story," he said.

"I got your title," I snapped at him. "Call it 'How I Gave Two Dogs Diarrhea.' Nobody'll steal that one," I muttered as I went back to the kitchen to get Sashi. Behind me I heard Harry and Reuben, voices raised, on the subject of canine care. I was coughing frequently by then; I had the energy to go home and that was it. On my way out I told Harry I was on sidekick sabbatical and he'd just have to get killed or ferret out the bad guy by himself until I recovered. Sickness calls off all bets, as far as I'm concerned. I'm just a big baby when I'm sick.

Carole Spangler stood in the foyer as Sashi and I walked out.

"I hope you—" I said, and hesitated.

"Choke?"

"I was about to say, work things out."

"Well," she said, nodding, "thank you. Maybe I will. Go home. Your face is turning green."

· · ·

I felt better but looked about the same when Joanne came to visit three days later in the late afternoon. When I heard the bell I thought it might be UPS; I'm always hopeful of getting a package. So I crawled out of bed and opened the door and there was Joanne, in her overcoat and cloche, in the foreground of a downpour. Her eyes were big, deep, very gemlike. She flinched a bit at my appearance.

"You drove down here in the rain?" I asked.

"I heard you were sick. I guess I heard right."

I invited her in and left her in the living room while I went to the shower. I was unshaven and still a little sweaty—not the way I'd wanted to look if she ever visited again. Things have to be just right for me to make a good showing.

I fixed the sweaty and unshaven part in the shower, and in addition got that temporary illusion that I was cured which a shower often provides. I half-expected her to be gone when I came out of the bathroom, but she was in the kitchen, having made some cream of broccoli soup which she herself had bought just before moving out and which had been in the back of the pantry ever since. We shared some in the living room, sitting forward on the couch, sipping.

"You were right about final read," she said. "There's a lot of pressure. I never realized until I had to do it regularly."

"You can do it."

"Well, I'm reading out loud now."

"Good. That'll help you on TV later."

"I know."

We sipped our soup.

"Harry said you stood up to Art Klee in London when he had a bow and arrow. What was up with that?"

"Well, it was no walk in the—well, wait, actually it *was* a walk in the park. We were over by Buckingham Palace . . ."

I went on, but I seemed to be telling it wrong. She kept staring at me oddly. She didn't even laugh at the Mr. Boffo joke.

"Harry also said you stood up for us with Easter," she said.

"Well, I said something to him, but it pretty much bounced off."

There was a pause.

"You've gotten skinnier," she said finally. "Bet you lost your handles."

"No, I don't think so."

I looked down at my stomach and she jumped on me. I fought back as best I could.

I can't say I had what you'd call a thought sequence during the next several minutes. We were busy to the point where I couldn't say there was any but the most basic thinking going on at all. And yet, at the end, by the time we wound up over by the TV set, I had reached a decision about our relationship. So there must have been some subterranean process taking place.

Joanne had jumped on me because of a rare relationship syndrome I'll call Man B Negative. What happens sometimes, when a woman leaves a man and starts up with another, is that the second man—man B—turns out to be a disappointment soon enough so that the woman may discover new or retroactive good points in man A. I'm not saying it happens often. On occasion, is what I'm saying.

Since our breakup I'd been acting differently, and Joanne had taken my behavior to mean that I had improved. Meanwhile, Ted Fairbanks had revealed himself to be flawed. What precisely he'd done I didn't know, except that Joanne later said his conversation was limited largely to how he looked, how he sounded and whether he should look or sound different tomorrow. Behind his back on the set they called him Ted Baxter.

Everyone knows luck is crucial. Had Joanne picked up with someone worthwhile, she never would have cared whether I was acting different or joining the circus. But because Ted was an oaf, I got one of Harry's second chances.

Now as I say, I didn't think this out while we were ricocheting off the living room furniture, but somewhere way under my predominant feeling I felt a little submerged layer of guilt. And as we lay on the rug afterward, this feeling fought its way up to a position of prominence. Joanne apparently admired me for the brave, uncharacteristic stuff I'd done after she left me. But I didn't feel like doing that stuff anymore. She was coming back to a guy who had only existed when she was gone.

We lay there, entangled, while I fought to get my breath back. Joanne got up first, blithe and refreshed. She retrieved and got back into her clothes while I remained flattened.

"You are skinnier," she said.

I managed to get up and start retrieving my own clothes.

"I'm not the guy you think I am," I told her.

She looked amused.

"Who do I think you are?"

"I think you think I'm different. But in London, I realized I'm really not. The only reason I've been more . . . active is because I went a little crazy when we broke up. But I've kind of come through that and now, here I am again. So in that sense, you just did it with the wrong guy."

She reacted philosophically.

"That may not be a first," she said.

She didn't seem upset. Maybe, as so often was the case, she didn't believe me.

Joanne said that Harry had come in to work for one day only, to invite everyone back to the castle for a party on that Saturday. An announcement was to be made at that time which everyone would find of interest.

He called me on Thursday, wanting to know if I'd seen Carole. She apparently hadn't been at the castle for two days.

"I'm a little worried," he said. "Reuben hasn't seen her either. She's been taking rides for Carpool Companions, which I've told her I don't want her to do. She said she wanted to get back out in the *field,* for Christ's sake. I said no, she goes out anyway. So she was calling in all right, but last night, nothing. So I thought I'd check with you."

"Nope."

"Wait, I got another call."

He came back on a moment later.

"It's okay," he said, relieved. "She couldn't get a ride south last night so she went to the office."

"Your office?"

"Yeah, she's got a key. I'm gonna go up and get her. Listen
. . . how are you feeling?"

I coughed, as I always do when anyone asks me that. "Fine,"
I said.

"Because it's time to wrap this up," he went on. "I'm calling
everybody to my place, just like what's-his-name used to do in the
old movies. The real old movies."

"Who, William Powell?"

"Yeah, yeah, the Thin Man. Everybody over to the castle. Tomorrow night. Be there or be square."

FIFTEEN

Harry had the castle all nice on Saturday. The unsightly burned-out wing was covered with one of those exterminators' tents, so the overall look of the facade was improved. He'd maxed out his credit cards to hire the help. His new housekeepers had the central and western sections spotless. Tables were set up in the theater/ballroom in front of the stage. There were security waiters; new caterers too. Savage was resplendent; his white coat was dazzling. He was everywhere. He loved company, just like Sashi.

I arrived at four; Harry had requested that I come early. He told me how he intended to address the staff. He also introduced me to the head of the security guys he'd hired for the night, a gentleman named Howard who was dressed as a maitre d'.

Harry's plan was simple but shrewd. After hearing it I agreed to stay, although I was a little apprehensive. It was designed to reveal the person who had caused Harry's accidents, and I thought it had a good chance of succeeding. After that, I had no idea what would happen, and I don't really like it when I have no idea what will happen.

Everybody from work showed up; it wasn't a full house, because you couldn't fill Harry's house, but it was full attendance.

Harry had also invited the core roster of Carpool Companions, since they were all living there anyway—Reuben, Stevie, Paul and Donna. I asked Stevie how Carpool Companions was going and he said okay except Reuben was an overbearing boss.

"He thinks he's Stormin' Norman."

Reuben himself was much in evidence. He had gotten a haircut and a shave and a safari jacket. He ambled easily through the building. He seemed serene. He nodded to me. Weekends were days off for Carpool Companions. He had nothing to do but have fun.

"Hey," he said to me out of the side of his mouth as we watched the caterers set up in the ballroom. "Is everybody coming from work?"

"I think so. That mention of an announcement should draw everybody."

"So Bobbi LaMott's coming."

I took a look at him. His eyebrows were hopping up and down like Jack Nicholson's.

Folks began trickling in at five. Some came right into the ball-room, which was off the big first-floor central living area; others wandered around briefly in the rest of the downstairs. I greeted them all, and they said hi back, coolly. The consensus seemed to be that I was not to be trusted. Eden Ramos came up and we did that head thing, the cheek press. She said, "You know what's gonna happen."

"No, not really."

Emily Hahn came over and looked around, wide-eyed and full of suspicion.

"Honey, I've got glaucoma. Tell me who that is over there."

"That's Reuben Schifrin. He does the Carpool Companions."

"Are we all gonna get our notice tonight?"

"I don't know." I didn't, either. Harry's plan had so many contingencies in it that I couldn't predict anything. "All I know for sure is that Harry's here, he's gonna talk, we're gonna have dinner, no tuna."

Ernie Scheffing arrived with his wife, Dorothy, but they didn't speak to me. Ernie and I hadn't had much to say to each other since he dimed me to five-0 back when Harry disappeared. Neil Purkey and Joanne entered together and came over to join me. We stood in the open area before the raised stage which faced the ballroom.

"So you went back to work for the big man," said Neil genially.

"Temporarily," I said.

Neil laughed.

"You're the only one who *isn't* temporary."

Joanne put her hand inside my elbow and faced Neil as part of me.

"He's a survivor, Neil," she said. "Deal with it."

Jimmy Nations and Steve Kluszewski didn't acknowledge me. Peter Hood said hi. Bobbi LaMott came in with Ted Fairbanks, but they weren't together. She walked away from him as soon as they entered the ballroom. Bobbi was taller than ever in her heels, striding forward, all business in a blue slinky dress, her eyes flashing, her cheekbones out like fins on a fifties car. She blew through everyone like they were swinging doors. Fairbanks was left behind with the extras. Some women are so pretty they make it rough on everybody. Reuben Schifrin came up to her and said something, or half of something; she was gone before he finished and he turned into a puff of smoke. Bobbi seemed to be looking for somebody.

She joined my little group at about the same time Carole Spangler did. I don't know where Carole came from; she just appeared, from the side. She was in her usual sweater and jeans, but her hair was dyed blonde and moussed.

"Hey," she said to us.

"Hey," said Bobbi.

"That's quite a look," I said.

Carole bent a knee and dropped a shoulder; did a little dip. "I didn't pierce anything. Want to stay just this side of Tower Records." She looked around. "Big night, huh?"

Harry hadn't been visible for a while. He'd gone to lie down. Now, as we found our name cards and place settings—my table included Joanne, Reuben and the Carpool Companions—he appeared on stage, speaking to one of his security waiters in front of the big TV screen upstage. Harry was elegant and imposing in a bulky white dinner jacket, starched white shirt and bulletproof vest.

I lost track of him as I found my seat, and saw him next on the ballroom floor, moving in my general direction, making his way among the diners, who were assembled eight to a table around the floor. The tables closest to the stage were reserved for the print staff so Harry could see them all clearly; the TV people sat farther back. Harry went to each grouping and said something, and seemed to get a civil response from everyone. On his last stop before reaching our table he greeted Bobbi, Emily, Eden Ramos and her husband, Neil Purkey, Peter Hood and the Ernie Scheffings.

He did a little polite sparring with this group and finally made his way over to join us, at the table closest to the stage. He put a hand on Carole's shoulder while addressing Joanne and me.

"She shocked me with this," he said, meaning the blonde hair. "I told her she's grounded."

Carole's eyes flickered slightly, but she said nothing.

Harry had not skimped on dinner, which I thought was gutsy on his part. He had already leased office space in a building in Santa Monica to start up *Second Chances,* and I don't think he had enough cash to treat us to Jiffy Pop. But we got salmon with asparagus and red potatoes. The security guards made excellent waiters. At our table, the Carpool Companions ate heartily, but I didn't have much appetite. Harry sat with Carole at a little table for two adjacent to ours, and attacked his salmon with caution. The *Who's Hot* staffers ate well generally, on the theory that there might not be a lot more meals coming from this source.

The combination of the food and the extra gear he was wearing made Harry perspire a bit. As the dessert—one scoop of mint chocolate chip—was served, he dabbed at his mouth with his napkin, then rose and made his way up the four steps to the stage and over to the downstage center microphone, which he tapped and removed from its stand.

"Hi, all," he murmured. He went through a couple of thank-yous . . . to the caterers and to everyone for coming from as far north as the San Fernando Valley.

"We've had our differences lately," he said. "Tonight we're going to resolve them."

The clinking and clattering of the cutlery stilled.

"As you know, I recently met with John Easter in London. Originally we were to meet in L.A., but I felt if I stayed around here I might not make the meeting. I had a series of mishaps which made me think that. Individually, each of these things could have been an accident. But they all occurred after I challenged you to stop me from selling the magazine. So . . . I got mad. By the time I left for London it was my intention, if I got my price, to sign you all over to Easter and kiss you off."

He looked them all over, and they all looked back.

"But on the way over I thought about it. And I spoke with Joe Hoyle here, whom most of you know. He said it was wrong to make everyone suffer for the actions of an unidentified pissant."

"That's a paraphrase," I called out, pedantically.

"I decided, too, that I owed you an explanation for why I'm selling. So here it is: I'm starting something up that's likely to operate at a loss for a while, and I can't get it off the ground without selling our shop."

Here Harry launched into an impassioned pitch for the whole *Second Chances* concept, comparing it to some of FDR's New Deal projects—I seem to recall the TVA and the Federal Theater Project—only with an entrepreneurial, self-help aspect included to appeal to conservatives. It was Harry at his most enthusiastic and persuasive, but it somehow fell short of gripping his audience. There were rustlings and rumblings. I think this was because the audience was made up of people who were going to be jettisoned in favor of the new program. To Harry's credit, he eventually caught on. He wasn't the kind of speaker who plows on endlessly, unaware that he's lost the house.

"All right," he said finally. "Maybe this'll cure your cough. When I first had this notion, I estimated I'd need twenty million dollars to get it started and keep it rolling. It came to me, though, during the early negotiations with John Easter's people, that he wanted *Who's Hot* pretty bad. And that he might be willing to pay more than twenty. More than twenty-five. Maybe thirty. And it occurred to me that I might share the surplus with the people who helped me make the magazine such a buy."

The rumblings stopped. In fact everything stopped. They weren't an audience; they were an oil painting.

"I decided that if I could get thirty million from John Easter, I would divide the extra ten among you, as a way of expressing my appreciation for your work over the years."

I love good oratory. Preachers, statesmen, comedians, salespeople . . . I love to hear somebody who knows how to talk. A good actor, too, can mesmerize an audience. It's a great experience, hearing someone capture the crowd. One recalls George C. Scott's opening speech in *Patton* . . . Burt Lancaster in *Elmer Gantry* . . . Bob Hope doing his "three against a thousand" story in *Fancy Pants*.

But Harry's effect surpassed them all. He'd say it was his delivery, but to me it was the content. He had the best material I'd ever heard.

As I looked around, I saw total attention. There wasn't a single face looking anywhere but right up there.

"As I say, all I hoped for, for myself, was the twenty million I'd originally earmarked for *Second Chances*. It seemed to me that with two hundred or two hundred fifty thousand dollars for each of you, I could leave you without concern. Ahem."

Having cleared his throat and looked keenly from one table to the next, he continued.

"Well, Joe and I met Easter. But before we could discuss price in any detail, he said, 'I hear someone's trying to kill you.' See, he'd found out about my accidents. Somehow." Harry looked around. "And it made him leery. He didn't want to bid on a plant with a ticking bomb in it.

"John told me that before we could settle on a price I'd have to resolve this situation. So I decided to invite you all here tonight. And here's my proposition: I think I can get thirty million from John Easter for *Who's Hot/Who's Not*, which means ten million for all of you. All I ask in return is some information. I want to know who poisoned me. . . ."

This was where I was supposed to be on the alert. Harry's theory was that no one would speak up, or point, but that someone on the ballroom floor might give something away while starry-eyed over that quarter of a million dollars apiece. I was to scan the faces at the crucial moment to see if anyone revealed anything: a flicker of fear of exposure, of guilt, of knowledge. Some trace of a reaction. A crack in the facade.

Well, I spotted one. Everybody looked at Steve Kluszewski.

． ． ．

I'm not saying they all spun in their seats and stared, although Ernie Scheffing's wife certainly did. It was just that, to a greater or lesser degree, almost the entire print staff felt compelled to glance over to the production table, directly across the floor from mine, where Steve sat beside Jimmy Nations. And Steve removed any doubt as to who they were looking at by leaping to his feet as if he'd been sitting in Harry's recliner.

"Sons of bitches!" he bellowed as his chair back clattered to the floor. "Fink narc pigeonshit . . . ! So I'm the fall guy. Who did the chair? Who did the jeep?"

"What did *you* do, Steve?" asked Harry from the stage. He hadn't required my help in catching the crowd reaction.

"I'll tell you what I did, you arrogant prick, I gave you that tuna," said Steve, in a voice quite free of remorse. "So you could see how it feels on the receiving end. You've been passing on bacteria as long as I've known you. They all know it. I told them all how you don't wash your hands after. I've seen you. You encourage people to come in when they're sick. The whole office is a germ culture, people coughing and sneezing up and down the halls. I brought home an infection that put my wife in the hospital. If I didn't get it from you, I got it from somebody who came in sick for you. You ruined my wife's health and undermined her lungs so she'll be vulnerable to respiratory infection for the rest of her life."

This all came out without stammer or pause. You could tell he'd thought about it.

"Are you sure about that, Steve?" asked Harry, doubtfully. "Seems like a stretch."

"I'd like to stretch you," said Steve, and stepped forward, into the space of uncovered ballroom between the tables and the stage.

As he stood before Harry, big and muscular in shirt and slacks, his lips compressed, breathing heavily through his nose, Steve was the embodiment of a type of guy I'd always dreaded—The Man with the Bug up His Ass. For some reason I'd always had a premonition that I would someday die at the hands of such a person— a person who felt I was on the wrong side of some dimly perceived or illusionary issue. Such people are spookier than the Art Klee type. You could understand Art Klee's position. Harry had made fun of him until he was enraged. Steve Kluszewski was different.

You couldn't quite follow his reasoning. You could only picture him at his desk, working it out.

Harry looked down on Steve from the lip of the stage. He twirled his hand mike by the cord a little bit while he listened. Steve was no clam. The words tumbled out.

"You're one of these bastards who spreads disease and doesn't suffer from it," he told Harry. "A carrier. I couldn't get you sick, man. I've coughed on everything on your desk. I hugged you and smeared E. coli all *over* you in the john after Art Klee came in that time. And you went on your merry way. You wouldn't go down! So I came to that picnic with some tuna—just a little bit; it smelled so bad I couldn't give you much, I had to disguise it. I did to you what you did to me. I had beef too, in case you switched back and ate that. I'd drive around with bad meat, bad fish. . . . I gave you bad meat once at work, stuffed it in a burger, but nothing happened. It was like a delicacy for you. You can't get Pigpen dirty. I was going nuts."

Harry was momentarily dazed. He'd received attacks on his person before, but not on his personal hygiene. Looking back, it did seem to me that, at least on the day of the paintball battle, Harry probably hadn't washed his hands after using the urinal. There might have been other times as well. I'd never paid attention. I knew a guy in college—not Harry—who said he didn't wash his hands after peeing because he didn't pee on his hand. Perhaps Harry shared this view.

But I could testify that Steve's portrait of him was wildly askew. I'd known Harry Poe for twenty years and he hadn't left any trail of diseased acquaintances behind him. Harry made people mad; he didn't make people sick.

"I'll put my cleanliness up against that of any man in this room," he now declared stoutly. "And with all due respect, your theory of the source of your wife's illness sounds to me like paranoid horseshit."

"Oh, yeah? Tell it to Claudia," Steve retorted hotly. "Do you have any idea how painful pleurisy is? I've become an expert. It's like a knife piercing your chest every time you inhale."

"Oh, yeah? Well, do you know how scombroid poisoning feels?"

"—fever skyrockets—"

"—your system completely shuts down to where you can't—"

"—twenty-four hours a day, delirium—"

"—swallow, breathe or even move your head without—"

"—fever, agony—"

"agony and indescribable—"

"PAIN!"

They didn't finish simultaneously, but they each got there. Kluszewski had a little better volume, but Harry didn't wither or retreat. He paced in a little circle onstage, then returned to the lip to address Steve again.

"Okay. You had some kind of even-up thing going on. But 'splain me this: When did I ever electrocute your wife?"

"No-no-no," corrected Kluszewski, who was now loosely surrounded by Harry's security waiters, moved in from the perimeter of the ballroom floor. "I didn't do anything after the picnic. Claudia talked me out of it. You want to know who shocked you, look elsewhere. All I did was the tuna. Maybe next time you'll wash your hands." He turned to address the rest of the staff. "Oh, and I want to thank you all for this—" He did a huge, exaggerated take, craning his neck around to look at the table he'd been sitting at with Jimmy Nations. "That was a champion sellout. You should all be very proud."

"Steve," said Harry, "I think the solution for you and Claudia is for you to work at home. For someone else." He gestured for his boys to see Steve out.

"So I'm fired," said Steve.

Harry laughed. "Needless to say."

"You're letting me go."

"That's right, Steve. 'Poisoned the Boss' will be your reason for leaving last job."

"And they all get money, and I don't?"

"Well, anyway, you don't."

The security men closed in on Steve, indicating the direction in which they wanted him to go—up the center aisle, between tables, and out the double doors of the ballroom.

"So what happens, I go outside and they kick the crap out of me?"

"We'd prefer to just walk you to your vehicle, sir," said Howard, the maitre d'.

Kluszewski looked Howard & Co. over. They were all bulky, with that kind of businesslike look.

"That's all right," he told Harry. "I got to see you go in the ambulance. I almost visited you just to see you on your ass, but I didn't want to give myself away. I still don't know how these finks all figured out it was me."

"It was tough," Joanne murmured. "After the paramedics left, he walks around muttering, 'Gotcha that time.' "

"And nobody said anything?" I asked her.

She shrugged. "Harry recovered." She grew restive under my stare. "Steve's a little scary, Joe."

"I could prosecute, you know," Harry was saying from the stage. "I'm giving you a break, Steve."

"Oh, I know what a great guy you are. You're all fine people. Jimmy . . ." He nodded at Jimmy Nations. "You're all right. The rest of you . . ." He looked around. "What can I say? To me you'll always be royalty."

I didn't see anyone blush. The only one to show concern was Eden.

"We'll need to hire somebody who can handle the system," she called up to Harry.

"I don't care," said Harry. "It's time we stopped saying he's a homicidal maniac but he's really good with the system. Expertise only excuses so much."

Kluszewski left, making it clear to the security guys that he didn't want to be touched by hands which had been who knows where. Everyone watched him out the door, and then the conversation in the room became general. Harry came over to the section of the stage nearest my table and squatted down to mutter, "Guy rubbed E. coli on me. That's gotta be new."

He strolled pensively back to center stage and addressed the rest of our group.

"This clears up one incident," he said, "but not the others. I want to know who's responsible for what happened afterward, on the Day of the Chair. The Day of the Jeep. If I can find out, I can assure John Easter that everything here is now shipshape, and I think I can get my price. Now I know none of you wants to be considered a snitch, so I don't expect anyone to name a name, or even point a finger. Just do what you did last time and that should be sufficient. Who's responsible for what happened to me that day?"

This time, there wasn't quite so emphatic a reaction, but it was discernible. A whole bunch of people looked at me.

SIXTEEN

It was the damnedest thing. I'd been sitting and watching, absorbed, at the end of the whodunit. Watching keenly, you know, to spot the guilty party. I was the last person I suspected.

But Emily Hahn was looking at me. Jimmy Nations and Neil Purkey were looking at me. *Joanne* was looking at me.

Harry sidled back over to the down right edge of the stage.

"Hey, Joe," he murmured. "What's goin' on?"

I had no idea. For a wild second I thought perhaps I had multiple personality syndrome. Maybe I hadn't done it as Joe, but as somebody else—"Gabriel," or "Freddie." But I had no history of anything like that.

"It's a frame, Harry," I insisted. "I didn't do it. I didn't do anything. I was *driving* the jeep, for God's sake!"

Harry grinned at me and quoted Fats Waller.

"Tell these fools anything, but tell me the truth," he said softly.

I didn't like the way he was looking at me; he had a reminiscent, Body Snatchers expression. I felt a little panic welling up.

"Goddamn it, I didn't do anything," I said, rising and bursting into a sweat. I certainly sounded guilty to me. I looked down at Joanne. "What are YOU lookin' at? You know I didn't."

"You gave us the idea," Emily Hahn said from her table.

I stared at her.

"That's not true," I said.

"You said we were making the magazine too attractive," she said.

"I—I—"

"You said *that*?" demanded Harry.

"I was—I was being sympathetic, one day, to the, to her, about the—you liar!" I finished, somewhat reprehensibly, glaring at Emily.

"You said we'd made it too attractive and that's why John Easter wanted it," she reminded me.

"I didn't tell you to fry Harry in his chair!"

"No, but I was discussing what you *did* say with a couple of people, and we thought—" She shrugged uncomfortably, and stopped. She seemed disinclined to continue. Harry scanned the room, waiting for someone to chime in, but his guests were studying the scrollwork on their plates.

"Okay," he said. "Let's wrap this up. I'm gonna offer amnesty on these other incidents. Just tell me what the hell happened so I can tell Easter we've recovered our poise here." He waited. "Emily." He rolled his index fingers over each other in a "let's go" gesture. "Come on. What went on in your head? What were you thinking of? You spoke to Joe and he said something brainless and destructive, and you then . . . ?"

Emily looked up at him warily.

"You said amnesty."

"Yeah, yeah," said Harry impatiently.

"Because I don't want to be forthcoming and then you renege on our benefits."

"If I don't hear something pretty soon you can all get whatever benefit you can out of my rear end."

Emily hesitated a moment longer, then plunged.

"After I spoke to Joe, I was at the coffeemaker with a couple people and we thought that maybe if there were problems at the office, and word got out about it, Easter might not be so inclined to buy us. Or maybe he wouldn't offer so much, and then you wouldn't sell. So what we did—"

She stopped, embarrassed. She seemed to be expecting someone else to come in on harmony.

" 'A couple people,' " said Harry.

"Well," said Emily, her voice trembling a bit, "I've said all I'm going to."

And she started rummaging in her purse. She was going to start smoking. I thought we might sit in silence for the balance of the evening.

"I guess this isn't gonna work," said Harry. "Pity about the money."

"Two practical jokes," said Neil Purkey suddenly, from his seat beside Eden Ramos. "Nothing life-threatening or. . . . Just enough so Emily could call Wesley Willis and tell him there was something going on here—you know, maybe the whole atmosphere wasn't so good. That the place wasn't such a value with a nut running around in it. It was pretty true; we already had Steve. And I'd read about Easter, how he'd had an incident with a guy stalking him. Figured he might not want to buy into a stalk."

Harry stared at him. "That's asinine."

"Excuse me," said Neil stiffly. "It worked."

Harry considered this.

"Well," he said after a moment, "it's certainly cold-blooded."

"Not like you," retorted Neil with some spirit.

Harry chuckled. He walked back toward center stage, shaking his head.

"Jokes," he murmured. "That electric chair gag was a good one."

"You said amnesty," Neil said quickly. "That was just bad luck; we didn't think you'd go that far—you know, through the air. We didn't want to kill you, except maybe for Steve. He did.

But we were just trying to make it look like . . . the place was unstable? Volatile?"

Harry nodded.

"Who all was in on this?" he asked.

"Oh, just really hardly anybody," said Neil. "Just me, and not
really Emily. I just developed the idea after she talked to Joe over
there, and that was about it."

"Hell with that," said Jimmy Nations from his table. "I yanked
your fuel fill line," he called to Harry. "So you'd run out of gas.
But I'll tell you, there were guys wanted to do more. They wanted
to jam you up real good."

"And who were they?"

"I don't remember," Jimmy subsided, moodily. "There was a
lot of kidding around. People can talk, I guess."

Harry regarded Jimmy indulgently. He always liked Jimmy.

"So who played with my chair?" he asked.

Bobbi LaMott laughed. Harry turned and stared at her.

"What are you laughing at—was it you?" There was another
pause. "Come on, people. We're almost home. I don't want to have
to differentiate between the people who spoke up and the people
who didn't."

"All right, it was me," called Ernie Scheffing, narking on himself for a change, despite his wife's whispered admonitions from
beside him. "Everybody's caving," he hissed back at her. "Better I
name myself than wait for somebody to name me." He spoke up
for Harry. "It was me and Neil. We made a little slice and pulled
out some of the wires, cut the insulation . . . We thought you'd get
a little jolt. We were just as shocked as you when you came into
the conference room with your hair all up like that."

"If you'd used any of the other settings it wouldn't have been
so bad," said Neil. "You must have pressed Ultimate."

That tickled Harry. "Where was my head?" he said agreeably,
rubbing the bridge of his nose.

It occurred to me that in an era where everyone spoke of serial killers, Harry had taken on the role of a kind of serial killee. He saw it too.

"So you've *all* been coming at me. It's like—" He snapped his fingers trying to remember the name and turned toward Bobbi LaMott.

"*Murder on the Orient Express,*" she said.

"No," said Neil. "Some people didn't want to go in. It was really more like *Mutiny on the Bounty.*"

There was silence on the floor. I looked at Joanne.

"Were you in or out?" I asked.

She shrugged. "I heard about it afterward. Everybody did."

"I'd like to say," called out Peter Hood, "that I had nothing whatever to do with it and I didn't hear anything about it and I'm appalled that it happened."

"Way to go, Peter, maybe you'll get the whole ten million," said Neil.

Eden Ramos spoke up.

"Harry, I think you've heard what you needed to hear. You can tell John Easter that the situation is resolved. And the amnesty is now in effect. Yes?"

Harry was twirling his hand mike thoughtfully.

"What? Oh. Amnesty. Well. Yes, absolutely. I don't see any reason why I should hold on to any resentment. A big man doesn't turn sour over a couple of pranks. The question is, does he reward them? Does he, upon learning his staff just this side of murdered him, then negotiate a huge bonus for each of them? Does he still get them that bicycle?"

Ernie Scheffing's wife slapped at his shoulder.

"Now you won't get anything," I heard her say.

"Do I understand you, Harry?" said Eden grimly. "You lied about the money?"

"Well . . . I'm considering turning out to have lied, yes," Harry admitted. "I'm mulling things over in the light of these revelations."

There was a pause while everyone reacted to Harry's treachery in his or her own way. I found myself watching Bobbi LaMott sit back from her dinner and put her napkin on her plate. She looked up at Harry and gave him a dazzler.

"I am SO glad you said that," she said.

Harry looked at Bobbi, a little warily, I thought.

"So what's next for Harry Poe?" she asked brightly. "Are you just going on to your new magazine with your new people? Or can we anticipate a change in your personal life as well?"

This question out of nowhere seemed to nettle Harry a bit. He cast a glance at Carole.

"There are some things happening," he said.

"Uh-huh," said Bobbi LaMott. "Is it the real thing this time, or is it like when you told me how, when your divorce became final, we'd get married?"

Now that's how oblivious I was when I worked there. I didn't know. Harry'd said they went out a couple of times, but I had no idea they'd become so close. Judging from the reactions around the room, I wasn't the only one to whom this was news. On reflection, I could see how it could've begun, and how it could've continued. Harry was taller than she was. She stayed late a lot.

Harry raised one finger to make a distinction.

"Now, no. I didn't say that. I said things would be different."

Bobbi LaMott laughed. Between her and Harry, it was a night of unsettling laughs and chuckles.

"That's good." She scraped her chair back and crossed her legs. "I must have misunderstood you the time *we* were on your recliner. When you said 'different,' you meant that if I'd be patient and wait, you'd eventually leave me for somebody else."

Harry eyed her narrowly.

"We're straying," he said.

"I don't think so. We're on the subject of keeping your word."

"Bobbi, we already had this talk." He held the mike down and lowered his voice to a murmur. "Why do you want to pick at it?"

"I've got something to give you," said Bobbi, rising from her chair and walking toward the stage.

As she reached in her bag, I stayed resolutely seated. Harry's security waiters were still out of the room, and there was a strong possibility that Bobbi was reaching for something dangerous—not a crossbow, not a paintball gun, not a Facer, but something. The potential for a crime of passion was there. But I didn't rise. I'd told Joanne I didn't do that sort of thing anymore, and besides, I thought that in this instance, Harry probably had it coming.

To my astonishment, however, Carole Spangler got up from her table near me and walked over to stand in front of Bobbi. Harry looked as amazed as I was.

"Don't," she said, as Bobbi rummaged in her bag.

"I'm gonna," said Bobbi.

She didn't produce a weapon, though—it was a videotape. She walked around Carole and held it up to Harry.

"Here," she said. "In lieu of notice."

Harry was so delighted at Carole's selfless behavior that he took the videotape without looking at it, or even noticing that he was taking it.

"Did you see this?" he called to me. "Did you see what she did here, when she thought I was in trouble?" To Carole he said, "There's a promotion in this for you."

Carole took a deep breath, shook her head and walked back to her table.

Harry now noticed the videotape in his hand and switched his attention to Bobbi.

"What is this?" he asked.

"You can play it later," she said, and turned away.

"Wait a minute," said Harry, looking at her darkly. "You're just gonna leave me with this and walk out?"

"Yup," said Bobbi.

"That's kinda gutless, isn't it? Don't you want to share it with the class? We could slot you in right over there and show it on the big screen."

"I think you'd be better off if you played it later."

Harry's eyebrows skyrocketed.

"Better *off*?"

"Well, you might not be able to—"

Bobbi looked up at him. They locked eyes.

"What?" said Harry. " 'Take it'?"

"This is tangential," said Eden Ramos from her table. "This is personal; it doesn't have anything to do with what we're all here for."

Harry ignored her.

"Lemme tell you something," he told Bobbi. "There is nothing you can say or do on this that'll make me break stride. I've heard it all before. You're the one with the problem. You had to make the tape because you couldn't face me with whatever you had to say."

Bobbi took a deep breath and stared at him.

"Okay, play it," she said. "I won't leave. I'll stand right here."

"Fine."

"Fine."

"What about the *bonuses*?" hissed Joanne, exasperated, while Harry walked over to the VCR on the offstage left side. "It's like we're not even here. Is he reneging or not?"

Harry put the tape in the slot, punched a couple buttons, the lights went off and a black-and-white image appeared on the big screen upstage.

The scene was Harry's office, from the POV of the security camera he'd had installed high up on the wall next to the entrance door. It showed all the files, Harry's desk and his recently repaired recliner.

For a moment I expected the tape to show somebody sneaking into the office and messing around with Harry's stuff. Instead, it showed two people in Harry's office, messing around with each other.

At first I couldn't tell who they were, but then I realized that one of them was Bobbi. I'd never seen her naked, of course. Nor had I expected to. Now we all did. After a few moments my eyeballs started to hurt, so I consciously blinked and tore my eyes from the screen momentarily to glance over at her. She stood at the foot of the stage and watched along with everyone else. She seemed comfortable with it.

I focused back up on the big screen, and then I made out who the other person was.

· · ·

Harry was a big thinker. Not a deep thinker, maybe, but a big one. And sometimes big thinkers are at a disadvantage. Sometimes, in his zeal to influence the multitudes, the big thinker falls short in the area of the individual relationship. When you're hovering over the planet, looking down at the general trends, you can lose track of the individual specks.

The other person in the video was Carole Spangler. She and Bobbi were on the recliner together, engaged in what the adult film industry refers to as a girl-girl.

The identity of Bobbi's partner was a shock to the room, but I recovered from mine sooner than most, I think, because as I stared at the screen I began to recall remarks Carole had made to me at one time or another that kind of meshed with what I was seeing. Well, let me amend that. I wasn't shocked at the *fact* of what I saw, exactly, but I was taken aback by the execution.

It was pretty steamy. You put the wrong two people on that recliner and it would have looked clunky, but Carole and Bobbi—especially Bobbi—looked confident and sensuous. Spontaneous, but smooth; not sliding off the chair or hitting their heads or anything. They really seemed compatible.

At first I'd thought it might be a joke. Carole had once suggested that she and I do something similar for Harry to see; I thought this might be a version of that. But the longer the scene ran, the less likely it seemed. They weren't stopping to wave.

On screen, Carole had blonde hair, so it must have been a very recent taping. I glanced over at her for a moment, sitting at the small table beside ours. She was leaning on her elbow with her head down and her hand shading her eyes. She seemed to sense my look and peeked up at me.

"I never photograph well," she said.

"No, you look good," I said. "No cellulite."

The tape was clearly a jaw-dropper for everybody in the ballroom, but there was no question who took it biggest. Harry had identified the two participants before the rest of us, since he was the only one to have previously seen both Bobbi and Carole in their present state. It hit him hard. It got right in under his vest. He wandered out to center stage and looked up at the screen, with the I-just-walked-into-a-glass-door expression he'd worn the night he found Carole in my kitchen. Actually, the glass-door reaction was pretty much universal, there in the ballroom.

Bobbi had moved forward until she was standing at the lip of the stage, just below Harry. She seemed completely at ease. I could never have acted with such aplomb while a roomful of people watched me naked on a big screen.

"You brought Carole up north so often, we used to get talking," said Bobbi as the tape continued. "Wednesday night after work she came into the office with her little Carpool Companions hat on and you know what she said? She said Joanne and I could be the female Siskel and Ebert. Really. Talking movies on TV like we do at the reception desk." Bobbi turned to Joanne and hand-mimed a phone to her ear. "I'll call you about it. It's a good idea."

Dorothy Scheffing had begun strenuously objecting to the show, and Harry finally managed to bestir himself, return to the VCR and eject the tape. The lights came on.

"Well, then we went out to a bar," Bobbi went on, "and at

the bar we got talking about you, Harry." She looked sunnily over at Carole. "Didn't we? And I was thinking that what you needed was a comeuppance. Like Tim Holt in *Magnificent Ambersons*. The whole town waits for him to get his comeuppance. And we got this joke idea, like . . . simultaneously! There may have been a drink or two contributing to it. And I have to admit originally it was, on *my* part, to get back at you. Pretty heavy revenge motive. I wasn't thinking of Carole too much then. And she said she had to do something spectacular to get through to you. So anyway, we went back to the office, because I thought: the recliner! Our spot, Harry, remember? We decided we'd shake you up." She gestured at the screen. "But you know . . . she's special. She's very giving. I think it shows. It started as a joke, and then it, like, turned into an experiment. And *then* it turned into a *successful* experiment, and now, I gotta tell ya . . ." She looked at Carole again. "I like her."

Harry took off his glasses and checked the lenses. He always looked vulnerable without his glasses.

"I guess this eighty-sixes my extra money," Bobbi concluded. "But it's all right. That money should, really, go to your homeless people. . . . I know you've got big goals. Carole and I'll be okay without it. We're starting this joint venture."

Harry walked stage right and stopped when he was even with our table, to look down at Carole. It was clear that despite his boast to Bobbi, her tape had broken his stride.

Reuben Schifrin's expression was eloquent as well, as he looked accusingly from Carole to Bobbi. Carole had preempted one of his best ideas.

Eden Ramos wanted to return to business.

"This is all irrelevant," she said from her table. "You wanted to know about your accidents, Harry. Now you do. Can we count on your word? A lot of people here heard it."

Harry sat down on the edge of the stage, still holding his microphone, and looked at the parquet floor.

"What about it, Harry?" called Eden. "Is the deal on?"

"Yeah," called Jimmy Nations. "And what about the amnesty?"

I could only grope for how Harry felt. I knew how it hit me when Joanne started up with Ted Fairbanks. I would have felt considerably worse if I'd come in to work and found everybody watching a video of Joanne and Ted in action.

Bobbi came over to where Carole sat, at the table for two.

"Ready?" she asked, smiling.

"You are a tough cookie," said Carole. She rose and came over to the stage, where Harry sat cross-legged, taking it in. She patted him on the knee.

"It's just so hard to get your attention," she said.

Harry searched her face.

"What about London?" he asked. "What about when we . . . ?"

Carole bobbed her head apologetically.

"It was kind of . . . Not," she said. "Sorry. Probably my fault."

Harry's face bleached out. She patted him on the side of it, then came back to our table to rejoin Bobbi. The two of them, a couple, stood side by side before Joanne and me. Carole Spangler's expression, while looking at Bobbi LaMott, was unlike any I'd ever seen on her. Before, she'd always worn a kind of dogged look, as if she were walking across the Great Plains. Taking advantage of the terrain, finding some water here, killing a prairie chicken there . . . surviving, but not arriving. Now she looked at Bobbi warmly, without self-consciousness or cynicism. And Bobbi, who could always pick and choose, looked down at her the same way. They both looked like they were set on Ultimate.

"Did we ever look like that?" Joanne muttered to me.

"Adios, Reuben," said Carole. "You can have the business."

"You've got some damn nerve," said Reuben. "Goin' after Bobbi when you knew I liked her."

"Why should men get all the babes?" she asked reasonably.

"Don't forget," said Bobbi to Joanne, "what I mentioned." She did the hand mime of a phone again. "It's a great idea."

I didn't exactly know what she was talking about, and at the moment I didn't care. The sight of Bobbi gazing down at Carole had finally exhausted my forbearance. As they started away, I rose and pursued them, circling until I faced them, blocking the center aisle.

"I can't let you out of here," I said, "without saying I'm shocked and offended."

Glowering at Bobbi, I ran my hand horizontally from the top of my head to well over the top of Carole's.

"If you're gonna have a rule," I said, "have a rule."

Bobbi laughed good-naturedly.

"Joe, this was special," she said. "We didn't know this was going to happen."

I stepped aside. I don't believe in belaboring a point and anyway Joanne was right there, but as a Hoyle I'm sensitive to infractions. Bobbi LaMott took *her own rule* and threw it down and danced on it. I'm not saying I was more attractive than Carole Spangler, but I'll go to my grave taller.

As I returned to my table I saw that Harry had disappeared from the stage. There was still confusion on the floor concerning the amnesty and the bonus money and the overall future of the *Who's Hot/Who's Not* staff, but it was not to be cleared up that night. You can tell the party's over when the lights go out.

SEVENTEEN

I didn't see Harry for some time after that. Not many people did. He holed up in the castle and ran *Who's Hot* by phone. I don't think he wanted to see anyone who'd been at the screening. Joanne kept me posted on the office news as long as she stayed there. I also got a report from Stevie, of the Carpool Companions.

Harry essentially kept his word on the amnesty, although he transferred Ernie Scheffing to the New York office, knowing that Ernie hated New York. And he promoted Neil Purkey to managing editor, thus ensuring that Neil would never have the nerve to give up his salary to try writing. He didn't punish Jimmy Nations or Emily Hahn. I don't know whether this was because he liked them more, or because he just ran out of retaliatory energy. Joanne said his leadership seemed to lose its punch after the party.

We'll never know what Harry would have done with that extra money from John Easter, because the deal fell through. When a Christian coalition boycotted the magazine in December over Christ coming in second on our Hot 99 list, a reporter called Harry for a reaction. His remark, "Ahhh, Christians, Schmistians," got a lot of unfavorable press. *Who's Hot/Who's Not* took a circulation hit. John Easter suspended negotiations for the sale in the wake of the bad publicity, even though Harry's accident situation had been wrapped up.

I ran into Stevie downtown one day and he told me that Harry had kicked the Carpool Companions out of the castle. Evidently, one day about a week after the party Reuben had come up to Harry demanding to know why there wasn't any cinnamon sugar in the house. Harry had said, "Why am I still looking at you?" The Companions were now operating out of the Barnacle Room, downtown.

During his farewell fight with Reuben, Harry had also said he was postponing *Second Chances*. Reuben accused him of quitting on the idea because Carole Spangler had left him, but Harry denied it. He said he'd just found out from his accountant that his homeless-only hiring idea was discriminatory. In order to function as Harry wanted it to, *Second Chances* would have to be a nonprofit organization. Here Harry had delivered five minutes of good stuff about how the nonprofit concept was an anchor on the human spirit and a denial of human nature and he'd be damned if he'd succumb to it. He was elaborating on this theme when everybody left.

The usual Harry, the Harry I knew, would have accepted the nonprofit challenge and found a way to circumvent it. But the man Stevie described sounded disinclined to try.

. . .

Harry took another hit—a big one, as it turned out—when Joanne gave him notice in order to review movies on cable TV with Bobbi LaMott.

This was the female-Siskel-and-Ebert idea Bobbi had mentioned the night of the party, the idea Carole Spangler got from watching Bobbi and Joanne talk film around the reception desk. She'd developed it on the flight back from London, a feminist concept which looked better the more you considered it: Joanne and Bobbi were vivacious; they both knew movies; and they ranged from attractive to blinding. Also, they had a nice built-in conflict that would play on TV, with Joanne as the skeptic and Bobbi the enthusiast.

Bobbi and Joanne got together and rehearsed their banter over the holidays at Bobbi's apartment in Santa Monica, where Carole now lived. And Carole, who had seen many a star at her dad's dental office, told them what looked most effective; she was creative consultant. In early January they submitted a demo to the local station that aired the *Who's Hot* TV show, and it tested quite well with both women and men. Bobbi and Joanne then taped three shows, which also tested well, and that's when Joanne gave notice to Harry.

She didn't have to give notice to me. We were seeing each other so seldom that we'd reverted to just-friends status without having to have a meeting about it. It didn't really hurt the second time; we had each concluded individually that we were right to break up the first time. I was able to congratulate her on the show without reservation, and I honestly looked forward to seeing it. I thought she'd be marvelous, exposing the eye jobs of the great and near-great, and I told her so. As a kickoff gift, I gave her a book of Pauline Kael reviews and another collection of the early work of Joe Bob Briggs. She seemed touched.

When Joanne told Harry about the new show he instantly became convinced it would be a huge success—mostly because it was Carole's idea. It was another example to him of her shrewd entrepreneurial instinct. He got to brooding about it.

•   •   •

As the new millennium began, I was dreaming regularly about being late for work. In one of these dreams I blew an interview with Orson Welles, who had come back from the dead to see me in order to drum up publicity for a film. I woke gladly, relieved to find I was merely unemployed. But as the day wore on the relief wore off. In waking life, merely unemployed was pretty bad. Harry had been right: I'd lost my venue.

Then one evening in late January I was watching the Yesteryear Channel, and David Dexter, the host, was taking phoned viewer requests for old films. Someone called in asking him to run the Cary Grant picture *You Can't Sleep Here*. Dexter couldn't recall any such film, and kind of blew the caller off. As it happened, however, I'd seen a studio flyer for it in London, so I sent an E-mail telling him that *You Can't Sleep Here* was the U.K. title of *I Was a Male War Bride*. I got a nice call back the next day from Dexter saying he'd read my stuff in *Who's Hot* and would I be interested in writing background material for him. I said oh, I don't know.

Well, I got up there to Culver City and half a dozen people there already knew who I was. The programming director, Sid Jaffe, told me, "You can write for David and the station magazine, but what I'd really like you to do, if you care to, is find hidden gems. Raise the dead. We've got the meat and potatoes, but we need garnish. Sterling Holloway anecdotes. Something about the Epstein boys, the twin screenwriters. Stories that haven't been told. People who haven't gotten enough attention."

There aren't many times in life when somebody orders you to do what you want. I told Sid about my Should've Been Hot list and he reacted as though I'd come over the mountain with the serum. He hired me on the spot and agreed to let me work from home two days a week. I asked for that so Sashi wouldn't be too lonely. She'd gotten used to my being home more.

I met a woman named Zoe there who said that an old *Who's Hot* article of mine, "Great Performances by Stars You Don't Like," actually changed her inner life. It got her to appreciate Jose Ferrer. She even took me out to lunch. She said our work is important. She was a little intense, but I found her very stimulating. I share her belief that good movies have curative, rejuvenating powers, although I think they're temporary.

I called Joanne to tell her about my new job and she sounded relieved. Turned out she'd been afraid I was going to fall through the cracks of life.

.   .   .

In February Emily Hahn called and told me I ought to go see Harry.

"He's very withdrawn," she said. "I thought he was all over it. He was coming in for a while, and now he isn't. I think he's drinking. Nobody's in charge here; Eden quit. He needs to snap out of it PDQ."

I went over to the castle on a Monday night. There was a "For Sale" sign out front; there had been since shortly after the party. No one so far, however, seemed to want to pay top dollar for a coliseum-sized building which was one-third burned down. The windows were dark except for one on the ground floor, facing the street. I rang the bell and nothing happened, so I went over to the window and looked in. Harry was sitting at one of the ballroom tables, his back to me, watching the big screen.

A pleasant surprise: He was watching the Yesteryear Channel. I had recently been given a great opportunity: Sid had let me set up a week of movies featuring people from my Should've Been Hot list. Harry was watching George "Foghorn" Winslow in *My Pal Gus*. I rapped on the window. He turned slowly and looked at me. I couldn't see his expression. Then he got up, also slowly, and left the room. I returned to the front door, hoping that was where he was headed. Presently he opened it and let me in.

He'd been drinking, and he, or the house, smelled bad. He didn't weave, but he walked very emphatically, as if he had to think about it.

He had a bottle of ale from a case John Easter had sent him, back when John Easter was interested. He offered to get me a bottle from the kitchen but I declined. Harry settled himself in his chair and I took a seat next to him.

"That's my movie you're watching," I said. "I picked it."

I told him about my new job, and Should've Been Hot Week.

"We're gonna have one whole night of movies with the Nicholas Brothers," I added.

Harry looked honestly pleased for me, and leaned over to shake my hand.

"Congratulations," he said. "You've finally become the most trivial person on the face of the earth." Then he collapsed back in his chair.

"What in the hell is the matter with you?" I asked him. "You were never a mope."

He shrugged.

"I could never soften her up," he said.

"Hey, she originally wanted to kill you. She DID soften up."

"You know, I burned that recliner."

"Harry, look at it this way: You lost her to a real knockout. That's no disgrace. At least you don't have to picture some *guy* with her. Move on. You're wasting your bonus time."

He was quiet for so long I assumed he wasn't going to respond. Finally he said, "That's the problem."

"What is?"

Harry looked up at the screen, and spoke slowly. Tentatively.

"I had this thought. . . . Maybe I got the bonus time . . . maybe I was saved that night in Chicago . . . not so *I* could do something, but just to set up somebody else. Maybe I got it just so I could live long enough to introduce those two. Maybe that was my whole mission in life: 'Carole, Bobbi. Bobbi, Carole.' And then they go on to become the Siskelettes."

I looked at him to see if he was serious and he snickered, embarrassed. He was legitimately struggling with this idea.

Once, years ago, as the guest of a friend who was a member, I attended a meeting of a Sherlock Holmes club in Chicago called, I believe, Hugo's Companions. These businessmen would get together semiregularly in a nice downtown restaurant and have a dinner in honor of Cónan Doyle's great creation. And there would be toasts, to Holmes and Watson and Irene Adler and even Moriarty, I think, and also one to "Stamford," because these gentlemen liked to toast. Stamford was the character in *Study in Scarlet* who introduced Holmes to Watson. That's all he did. That was the only scene he had. After he performed this service, he disappeared forever. And no one remembered him, except the most dedicated toasters.

This was the idea which had attacked Harry—that he might be a Stamford instead of a Holmes. A spear-carrier. An anonymous catalyst. And he hadn't been able to shake this new angle on his bonus time. Coming on top of his public jilting, it struck at the core of his understanding of life. Life only made sense to Harry if he was central to it. He had always assumed that we didn't go over the rail back in Chicago so he could go on to greatness. Now the thought had insinuated itself into his mind and wouldn't go away: Bobbi, Carole. Carole, Bobbi.

My Pal Gus ended. Next up was Clu Gulager in *The Killers*.

"You're going to end up with seventeen viewers," Harry commented.

"Seventeen discriminating viewers."

"I suppose *you're* going to amount to something now."

"Nah, I don't want to be in the spotlight. I just want to *work* the spotlight."

He gazed at me blearily.

"Hell, maybe it was you," he said. "Maybe we were saved so you could be a crusader for film preservation."

He got up and walked back out toward the kitchen. I followed him, careful not to trip over clutter in the half-light. The smell out there was worse; even Harry noticed it.

"Smells like crap out here," he muttered. "I need to get some help."

"You need to stop slopping around," I suggested. "You're the only genius John Easter ever met in California, remember?"

Harry stepped up into the kitchen and grabbed a six-pack of ale off a counter. "I'm a Used to Be Hot. I'm a Where Did He Go."

Something in the corner of the kitchen caught my eye.

"Hey," I said.

I walked over to the little nook under the cutting board and squatted down to get a better look.

Savage looked back up at me, meek and depressed. He didn't raise his head; only his eyes. His coat was matted and dirty. He'd licked a "hot spot" onto one of his paws. I glared up at Harry, who stared foggily down at me.

"This dog has been neglected," I said. I got up and started looking around. I walked down the steps from the kitchen into the dining area, and over toward the back wall.

"It's around here somewhere," I announced, sniffing. "Turn a light on before I step in it."

Harry flicked a switch and I found it. I also found a chair which had been tossed up against the back wall.

"His doggie door has been blocked," I said. I turned to face Harry, who stood, dully mortified, in the kitchen.

"I threw the chair last night," he said. "I was trying to spontaneously release my pain."

I came back up the steps to the kitchen area.

"Lemme spontaneously release something in your direction. This dog had to shit indoors. That's why he's under there. He's embarrassed. And he's licking his paw because that's how he bites his fingernails. You know how a fastidious dog feels if he has to do it in the house?"

"Okay, okay." Harry crouched down and took Savage's head in his hands.

"Look at that, his ears are down," I said. "He thinks *he* did wrong. He doesn't know *you're* the ass."

"Are you gonna give me a lecture on dogs?" He stood up, truculent. "Are YOU gonna lecture ME? I had Savage before you even *dreamed* of getting Sashi."

Under the cutting board, Savage wore the glum, despondent look that kids get when their parents are arguing over their heads. Harry glanced at him and shut up as his guilt kicked in. I think Harry's ears would have gone down too, if they could've. He crouched down again and ran his hand over Savage's muzzle.

"Here's a bonus time theory," I said. "Maybe you were saved so someday you could provide Savage with an unobstructed god-damn doggie door."

As I headed out, I heard Harry clamber to his feet behind me, and his footsteps following. He caught up with me in the foyer and put his hand on my shoulder. I turned around.

"Thanks, Joe," he said simply. "I prefer your interpretation."

· · ·

As I write this, Harry Poe has returned to *Who's Hot/Who's Not*. Emily says he came back polite, which she finds unnerving.

Polite may not be right for Harry. I hope he rediscovers him-self. I think he's still capable of doing some great thing. That's his style, to paint with a wide brush. He wasn't meant for detail work, and he's rarely sensitive to the person across the table, whoever that may be. But at his best—thinking big, or facing irate actors with weapons—Harry Poe has few peers. Now that I don't see him so much, I appreciate him more. He's troublesome in the present tense but enjoyably vivid in retrospect.

The image of Harry I treasure most is of him in St. James's Park, telling his joke to Art Klee. I don't know anyone else who could have carried that off. Or would have had to.

As for me and *my* bonus time . . . Should've Been Hot Week went well, and I got to set up another. I called my old actor friend Marty Best and told him we were going to feature one of his movies, *Get Out of Dodge*, and asked him if he wanted to come in and introduce it with David Dexter. He said sure, sounded all tickled about it. Then Sid Jaffe said *I* could introduce it with Marty. He said he liked my enthusiasm.

So we did that, and now Sid's thinking of giving me a little semi-regular segment where I introduce underrated films. He wants to call it According to Hoyle. Zoe's going to direct me so I come off a little better on camera. They're even going to buy me a blazer. Zoe took me to lunch again yesterday.

It's an amazing thing. They think I'm—well, not hot stuff, exactly. But for the first time in my life, I'm getting warm.